Shena Mackay was born in Edinburgh in 1944 and educated at Tonbridge Girls' Grammar School and Kidbrooke Comprehensive School. She left at the age of sixteen and has worked at a variety of jobs – as an artist's model, a library assistant, for a herbalist, and in a greetings card factory and an antique shop.

Written at the age of seventeen, Shena Mackay's first novel, *Dust Falls on Eugene Schlumburger/Toddler on the Run* (1964) was published to critical acclaim, as was *Music Upstairs* (1965). Both are published by Virago. *Old Crow* appeared in 1967 and was followed by *An Advent Calendar* (1971), *A Bowl of Cherries* (1984) and *Redhill Rococo* (1986), which was awarded the Fawcett Society Prize. Her latest novel is *Dunedin* (1992). She has also published two collections of short stories, *Babies in Rhinestones* (1983) and *Dreams of Dead Women's Handbags* (1987). Some of her short stories have been broadcast and they have also appeared in a variety of magazines and anthologies.

Shena Mackay is also a book reviewer and journalist. She has three grown-up daughters and lives in London.

OLD CROW

SHENA MACKAY

Published by VIRAGO PRESS Limited 1992
20–23 Mandela Street, Camden Town, London NW1 0HQ

Reprinted 1992

First published in Great Britain by Jonathan Cape Limited 1967

Copyright © Shena Mackay 1967

The right of Shena Mackay to be identified as the author of this work
has been asserted by her in accordance with the Copyright, Designs and
Patents Act 1988

A CIP catalogue record for this book is available from the British Library

Printed in Great Britain by Cox & Wyman Ltd, Reading, Berks

To R. F. B.

Chapter One

Not old Mr Thompkin with the kindly white hair?

'So you do understand why we can no longer have you in the choir.'

'Yes.'

* * *

On a hot windy day in 1958 cutting grass lashed and lashed in the field below the cottage. Coral said, 'I have been asked by Mr Thompkin to leave the choir because of my association with you,' and Paul Brick, a painter of no reputation staying near the village for the summer, laughed. She turned from the window and bent her head to plunge a grey surplice into the mound of rainbow bubbles doubled by a tear-filled eye. Paul was redecorating her father's cottage; he dropped the brush into a tin of whitewash and came over to the sink.

'Let's give them something to talk about then.'

'At least I shall leave behind a clean surplice, if a dirty memory,' she cried as she ran out of the room. When she came down again Paul laid his scrubby beard against her cheek and suggested they went for a walk when he had finished for the day.

They walked across stiles and stony fields to a plum orchard where hard yellow and soft purple plums lay blown and muddy under the trees. Wasps in the cooler air buzzed on the rotting fruit and horse-flies hovered and feasted where cows had walked.

'Oh, look at the lovely mauve sky,' sighed Coral. How complacently the juice dribbled through her square white teeth, and she turned displaying pink clover prints on the backs of her plump knees. 'And the clouds. Sometimes I lay in bed and imagine I can see all pictures in the stains on the ceiling.'

'And can you?'

She swamped a dandelion with her blushing face. The grass felt cold to her fingers and the purple was fading from the sky. Fields and silence stretched for miles around. He lifted the hair gently from the back of her neck and pulled her back and she screamed harshly to the flints and dead electric fence. She had lumps of dry earth in her hair and a venomous baby nettle under her leg. On the way home she found someone had switched on the fence and she jumped back with a jangling arm and thought she heard mocking laughter from a barn on a hill a mile away. It echoed round the empty field and was joined by Paul's and the sound of church bells and she started to run and ran all the way home past clutching brambles and goose-grass and her father nailing a crow to a post in the garden and up to her bedroom. Some hours later she pinned the last pink roller into her hair and entered a figure 1 in her diary. Outside in the wind dry wings flapped on wood.

Paul wandered back to the village, pausing to take a green and red stone from a spring and watch it turn brown in his hand and to pick up a giant Roman snail from the beaten mud path and put it in his pocket. He called in at the King's Arms and found Coral's mother leaning on the bar, her elbows coming to fat points under her short-sleeved dress, and bought her a drink.

In the morning he found unhappy little trails of slime down his trouser leg, across the floor to the door where the snail lay exhausted with bits of fluff bubbling and foaming in the opening of its shell. He cooked himself a sleazy egg, picked at a nodule of paint off the easel standing like a little gallows in the corner, and set off for work.

Chapter Two

He was not alone in the house; a white moth hung in the fold of a curtain, chrysalises and eggs lay wrapped in a web in the corner of the window-sill which was painted the same sour green as the nettles outside, a spider was splayed like a stain on the rusty bath. Above the breath of insects in the silent house he heard the swish of wheels and the gate being pushed against long wet grass. Coral came in with her hair beaten flat against her head and emptied a pool of water from a cracked white shoe. He plucked at her sleeve, but she pushed him off and sat down. Rain rolled down the window and a fly buzzed in the dry mouth of a squeezed lemon.

'To what do we owe this unexpected pleasure?'

'To your stupidity.'

Then she jumped up and placed her wet head against his chest and he realized with distaste that she had come to place her fat life in his hands and he picked up a knife. Coral looked up from picking at her nails and saw his hot mouth twitching in his beard. She hooked her shoe on with her foot. He scratched his chest with the tip of the knife and stared at her. She gave a little scream trailing into a giggle, rushed out of the house and down to the gate with him after her, dragged the bicycle across the grass and mounted. He grabbed it from behind.

'Just a minute. I'll fix everything,' he babbled, giving her saddle a reassuring pat and sending the bicycle bouncing over the flints and down the hill.

Tensely stuffing whole pilchards into his mouth from the tin he stared through the thick glass at the rain. The tap dripped loudly in the shallow sink and outside tall grass was dripping under the grey sky. Suddenly he roared and pulled a bleeding finger from his mouth. He threw the tin across the room and started down the road to the pub.

Pilchards were tossing in a sea of cider. He leaned on the bar and looked down. Among the polished shoes and rubber boots a pair of gross bare feet sprouted from sandals which he recognized as his. He left the pub and flapped along the street towards Coral's house past gardens with drops hanging from the gates and black earth smelling of rain and night-scented stock. He paused to stroke a rose and snuffed out an earwig between finger and thumb, walked on a few yards, then stopped. On the stone bridge, with their backs to him and legs swinging out over the river where beds of green weed wavered in the shallow water, sat three girls, the middle one Coral, with their arms linked. Her hair blew out and subsided on her shoulders and their mouse curls stirred as a last scattering of raindrops hit them. Paul set off at a gallop up the road, and round the corner flung himself panting against a wet privet hedge. A surprised insect flew into his mouth and drowned. He saw a bicycle and seized it and started to wobble home but was soon forced to dismount by the mild slopes of the hills. He shoved his clothes and paints into a bag, said good-bye to his easel, hung the bag over the handlebars and climbed on to the bicycle. With a thrust of his foot he flew down the road, dragging on the useless brakes, his sandals hanging over the pedals, the bag bumping and swerving the handlebars, over the gravel and stones and dead birds which were many at that time of the year, with the broken rear mudguard sending a stream of mud and grit on to his back. When he reached the level high street he tried to pedal but the chain scraped rust on the ground and the pedals spun uselessly.

'Get off and milk it,' shouted a voice. He could see no one. He dragged his bag uneasily through the village to the station. On the platform he slipped on a wet chestnut leaf, nearly falling on to the line, but recovered his balance in time to board the London train.

* * *

Coral clutched the edge of the dressing-table in a mist of sweet peas and lavender polish and stared at the flesh that had brought this fate upon itself.

'Coral,' roared a voice from downstairs. 'Get on that bicycle you're so fond of and find out what that so-called artist friend of yours thinks he's playing at and whether he intends to condescend to finish the job or if he expects me to pay him for nothing.'

'What shall I say, Dad?'

She pushed open the door and stepped in and floundered in the stale silence of the empty house. Her mouth fell open and when she closed it a second shocked chin hung round her throat.

Chapter Three

'It's the chance of a lifetime,' said Mr Fairbrother, wondering what the prospects were for an old fool. The blue air letter fluttered in his thick fingers as he handed it to Coral, and she read her emigrant brother's offer of the fares to Australia for a holiday if not for a lifetime.

'That's great. When are you going?'

'You too, dear,' said her mother.

* * *

Six long weeks later Coral watched the green train disappear leaving her in silence to brush away a fly from her eye and stare along the track into a haze of midges, with her hand soaking the paper with its headline.

LOCAL FOLK GO DOWN UNDER

Sometimes in the edgy silence she would see haggard faces in the hedge, hear scratchy voices through the thorns, rush out to confront them to find perhaps an old lady talking to the sparrows or nobody.

It seemed to her that she went to bed one night a village beauty and rose the next morning a laughing stock, but the transition was more subtle. The story of her downfall started at morning surgery on a misty November 5th, when the smell of wet leaves and gunpowder hung about the streets, and burst fitfully round the bonfire in the Recreation Ground that night and was absorbed into the general consciousness. Nobody was surprised except all the boys.

A few mornings later she was sitting watching television with a plate of biscuits on the arm of her chair and a slaty little fire spitting in the grate. Her hand slid across the surface of the empty plate. She shook the biscuit packet and found there was no food in the house, so she stuffed a handful of cold hawthorn leaves into her mouth and strolled into the village. A postman in a cape and leggings sent dirty water from his front tyre as he cycled past. There had been no news from Australia for several weeks. She drifted into the music-filled doorway of the King's Arms almost without noticing and emerged two hours later from the warm brown room as the sky cleared. She stepped off the pavement into a woman on a bicycle and they crashed in a tangle of wheels, legs, arms and baskets. A car skidded in a shower of grit and bumped against Coral's shoulder and she saw her head roll a little way down the road and lie staring at her from the gutter and fainted. When she opened her eyes she was staring at a feather floating down a stream of dirty water until it was swirled to a drain and battered against the bars and bent and was sucked under. She was sitting on the edge of the pavement with her head between her knees and she raised it as her opponent retrieved a dripping drumhead cabbage from the gutter. They parted shamefacedly and, one wobbling with a twisted wheel, the other limping, fled the little crowd that had gathered.

*   *   *

'No long spaghetti? Well, the other kind will have to do then. I wonder if you can help me?'

The grocer looked up from packing down a bag of potatoes on top of the eggs she had bought elsewhere.

'I wonder if you can recommend someone to help me in the house, general cleaning and so on? Fairly clean and efficient if possible,' she laughed.

Mr Fisher knew the house well, until recently it had been a tied farm labourer's cottage occupied by his brother-in-law. It had been exhaustively repaired and redecorated and 'The Shambles' had appeared on its gate.

'I'll let you know if I hear of anybody, madam,' he said, scratching a greasy furrow in his hair and replacing the pencil behind a vast ear.

* * *

Joan Blake had her hand on her gate to open it when a voice said: 'Excuse me,' and she turned to face a girl standing like a bronze chrysanthemum against the November sunset.

'I heard what you said in the shop,' she said from a mud-splashed face; 'that you wanted someone.'

'Yes. Well you'd better come in to the kitchen.'

Coral smelled of warm beer among the white tiles; her brown hands lay in her lap and mud-streaked hair fell on to a brown shoulder as drizzle clouded the leaded window-panes. Yellow apples spilled from a bag on to the scrubbed pine table as they talked. Coral picked one up absent-mindedly, polished it on her skirt and ate it entirely as they talked. When she left she found that news of her accident had preceded her and that she was to be without dignity.

*   *   *

Dennis Blake came home from work to find his eleven-year-old daughter Clare with her back to him at the window-sill dismembering a moth. His red ears stuck up coldly on either side of the little bowler he wore.

'What on earth are you doing?' he asked, removing his hat, knowing better than to expect a welcome.

'It's for school.'

'But you're doing plant biology.'

He opened the window and knocked out the remains.

'Guess who's coming to work for us, Daddy?'

'Black Beauty?' he asked hopefully, knowing she liked horses.

'Who?' she asked and he feared he had gone too far but she went on: 'It's that fat woman who lives by herself in that dirty house with the chickens. She's absolutely vile.'

And father and daughter departed towards the kitchen in search of food.

Chapter Four

'Comb your hair across your pate dear, we're off to the horspital.'

'You go on, I'm not coming.'

'Not coming to see Coral's baby? Your own great-grandchild?'

'No.'

'Well all I can say is don't let me find you here when I come back, that's all.'

When she came home she found he had moved into the tiny toolshed on his allotment where he stayed wrapped in sacks for two weeks until the almshouse for which he had put down his name fifteen years ago fell vacant. He had left behind Trixie, their wee fox terrier.

'There is a ban on animals in almshouses,' he wrote in his farewell letter, 'so you will not be able to visit me.'

She often passed him in the street, an upright figure in cycle clips and cap.

Four years ago Mr Fairbrother had placed a brown-and-white puppy, which he had found shivering in the icy grass at the allotment gate, in his wife's lap, with a winter cabbage. It slid down her leg tearing her peach lisle stocking.

'No,' she said, clamping her gums shut. Mr Fairbrother threw a bloody parcel of meat on to the table.

'I'm going to have a bath,' he said.

'It's not your birthday, is it?' replied his wife.

The next hour, while he filled the tin tub and scrubbed himself with the black-veined yellow soap, set a precedent for years to come. Trixie, as she came to be called, laddered Mrs Fairbrother's other stocking and nipped her hand so that a round purple blister formed at the apex of her tissuey finger. When Mr Fairbrother reappeared she was curled up in the best chair. Had they ever had visitors they would have been forced to stand.

Since he had gone the evenings seemed long with the television constantly accompanied by a dismal whine. Should she creep back to bed in the morning with an indulgent cup of tea, she would end up on her knees in her nightdress mopping a stream of tea leaves from the pillowcase and wall; let her raise a lump of cream to her lips and an acrid snout would thrust into her face, she would lay the cream by for later, and as often as not it had been devoured when she came for it or had gone sour.

Trixie came loping through the twilight with an oven-ready chicken. Mrs Fairbrother sighed as she watched her eat it and wondered if she would visit her grand-daughter again, but the bed was due to be vacated in the morning.

Chapter Five

Ice muck and straws clogged the gate as she pushed it open with one hand, the other clasped a white bundle. The taxi drove away. The back door opened on a house unchanged but for a week's growth of dust; damp suffused from the wallpaper into the dark little room. She placed the baby in the cold frilled nylon of the cot and gave it a rock. Then she crumpled a week-old newspaper and lit it and added a few sticks dotted with red lichen. When the cold flames died to crinkled ash she took the baby, whose eyes were still closed like the seams along broad beans, and crept into bed. It was ten o'clock in the morning.

* * *

Joan Blake pulled out the plug and lay stranded like a whale in the bath, watching steam condense on the frosted glass and run down the window while the drift on the window-sill grew slowly higher and blocked the yellowish light. She pulled on the cord that switched on the light and stood upon her thin legs with round over-hanging knees.

'I thought you might come and scrub my back,' she said to Dennis in the sitting-room.

'How could I with this cold?'

She sighed and clicked a lighter at a cigarette.

'Are you going back to work tomorrow?'

'If the weather clears. And if I don't feel as rotten as I do today.'

She had run the little vacuum cleaner round the floor and felt exhausted.

'I wish Coral would hurry up and come back.'

'Clare doesn't.'

'Oh Clare!' she said, but thought of her daughter at school in the snow as the anthracite in the grate glowed and later that afternoon pecked at her forehead with the usual panic that the wrong hat and blazer had got into the car.

'Look Clare, your mother's said she was sorry. She was pleased to see you, that's all. I'm pleased when I see you – we're your parents, Clare.'

They sat side by side on the oak settle, the Mongolian rug frothing round their feet, until Clare banged her bedroom door behind her.

'Think I'll look in at the King's Arms, if you don't mind,' said Dennis.

'What about your cold?'

'I'll take it with me,' he said buttoning his coat and tucking his trousers into a pair of boots. When he got out he found that the snow had stopped and was hard beneath his feet as he walked on black shadows on the road. He entered the pub and threw out a hearty greeting.

'Good evening sir,' said the landlord.

'The usual, Jim.'

'What's that, sir?'

He took his drink past the group of farmworkers and

stood a little way down the bar, and got joylessly drunk, pouring down his throat glass after glass of beer as cold and wet as the water slapping against the mud walls of the river outside. He began to think about his wife's help bending with a dustpan on the tiny stairs in a dress of coarse blue poppies on a white field. He remembered in detail a melancholy week-end in Bournemouth he wished to forget and stood flushing at the bar. After a slight scuffle at the top of the stairs his secretary went in front of him into breakfast. Their little table was beneath a cuckoo clock whose hands said ten past four. The cuckoo squeaked the quarter. Dennis took the opportunity to meet her eye and smile. Across the room a gruff voice ventured to offer toast.

'Jolly nice breakfast,' whispered Dennis.

'Mmmm.'

A bee buzzed against the french window somewhere by the table legs.

'What is it?'

She bent down and he saw a cobwebby white vest as her white cardigan rode up her narrow back.

'A bumble bee.'

'Stupid creature.'

'More tea?'

'Thanks.'

'I don't take sugar.'

'I beg your pardon?'

'I said I don't take sugar, but it doesn't matter.' The cuckoo gave a weak croak.

'He's off again!'

'What?'

'I said, he's off again.'

'Another cup?'

'Not for me thanks. You?'

'I think I'll have just half a cup.'

Dennis placed a hand on the teapot.

'Which half would you like?'

'Last orders,' said the landlord.

As he pushed the snow along the top of a wall with his hand Dennis encountered a bush of battered jasmine. He tore off some branches and carried them with him. The idea he had been suppressing most of the evening came to the forefront of his mind, and with swift cunning he removed his boots and tiptoed past his gate in his socks and when in safety replaced them and ran through the unlit street past scarcer houses until he was at Coral's gate with the moon racing past and blood thundering in his head. He knocked on her letter-box and waited. 'Come on, come on, come on,' he sang through his teeth.

He rattled it again and waited, black seconds thudded past. He placed his mouth to the letter-box and shouted:

'I know you're in there.'

He could see her clutching her wanton sheets about her.

'Open up.' He shouted and beat the door with his fists.

'Come down here! Open the door, it's me!' he coaxed in a screaming whisper, crashing the knocker down. The silence of the corrupt country beat round him, then from an upstairs window came a broken wail like a lamb in distress. Dennis laid down his jasmine on the step and crept up the garden.

He got home to find an anxious figure quietly putting on a coat to come to look for him. As he sought forgiveness in her woolly shoulder he was shaken by a fit of shivering, and the following morning Coral shut the kitchen door to muffle her baby's cries as she sponged spilled coffee from the tray she had brought down from the bedroom where Dennis lay confined with a heavy cold.

Chapter Six

Cow parsley simmered in the boiling grass and the bitter smell of elder trees hung over the hedge. The black pram outside the back door had lost its hood and mudguards; in the five years that had passed a little girl in glasses squatted beside it rubbing sorrel into a rusty pot and a few feet away a boy of about three was playing with a milk bottle. Cabbage whites fluttered in the glare above torn and frilled cabbages, black and white bean flowers burned on stalks that were shimmering columns of insects and beyond them four ragged hens scratched the baked floor of their run. Coral came out of the house, looked into the pram, and flopped down in the grass, and later shuffled down the lane to the shops without looking at the poster that announced a Parish Council meeting the following evening.

* * *

'Paula Fairbrother's absent again,' said Miss Jigger, running a finger across the row of black noughts that disfigured her register. She handed the register to the headmaster and pulled off the sailcloth smock, casually daubed in places with the brighter powder paints, which she affected.

'Something will have to be done,' she said, but she

had no time to discuss it then as she hoped to catch the train in time to have a look at some pictures by that new man Brick before going to a Polish film. Mr Gutteridge saw a deep groove under the name as if a cruel thumb nail had often lingered there.

'I'll get on to Evans,' he said.

'Will you? Why?' she asked, rubbing the lipstick off a molar with the corner of a handkerchief.

'He's the Attendance Officer.'

'Oh. It's the parents I blame, of course.'

If so, thought Mr Gutteridge, why deal so savagely with the children?

'You look very posh tonight, Miss Jigger. Going anywhere special?'

'Oh well actually I ... '

'All dressed up and nowhere to go eh? Never mind. We appreciate you,' he misinterpreted, waving an arm at the untidy desks and his greasy tweeds had gone before she could explain. In her rage she seized and tore in pieces the nearest thing to hand, which was somebody's sum book.

* * *

Filston Parish Council sat round the table on the stage of the corrugated iron village hall; one of the little windows had been forced open to let in more heat and the rest of the hall was filled with rows of empty wooden chairs. The minutes had been read and those members who had resigned last month had been reinstated.

'It is agreed then that we enter Filston for the Best Kept Village Competition,' said Stella Oates, who sat well back in her chair so that her little feet in linen shoes would not touch the ground, 'and that the main obstacle in our path to the winning post is Miss Coral Fairbrother.'

There were signs of agreement from all but the newest member, the almost disillusioned Dennis Blake.

'That woman,' she went on, 'owes me, let me see' — she placed her neat white head in the opening of her bag and took out a red notebook — 'three shillings and sixpence for the Parish Magazines.'

Mr Masters coughed. 'I'm afraid, Stella, some of us are not altogether blameless in that respect.'

She laid a tiny white-gloved hand on his arm and the meeting continued.

'Couldn't they be rehoused on the council estate?' suggested Dennis.

'Nothing available, besides they'd wreck the place. No, that house is a slum and an eyesore and must come down, fast. And if not it will have to be thoroughly re-decorated, outside, and the whole garden dug up and replanted, or perhaps we could throw some rubble on it to make it look like a rock garden.'

'What do you intend to do with the family? You can't repaint them or throw rubble on them,' said Dennis.

'Put the children in a home, run the mother out of town and slaughter those mangy chickens.'

'I wonder what she does with those parish magazines; totally illiterate you know.'

'She used to be a secretary,' said Dennis.

'My God!'

Dennis rose and left the meeting and hurried through

the village. The door was opened by a boy in a washed-out pink nightdress above his knees.

'It's about my job,' sighed Coral over the sound of the unlicensed television, and she sank back into a chair. Paper peeled from the walls and a spongy fungus grew under the window-sill. The little boy climbed on to his mother's knee and she carried him upstairs, and Dennis, curious to see the rest of the house, followed. A space gaped in the chest of drawers; the drawer was on the floor between two beds and a baby slept in it. Dennis recognized one of the beds; he had seen it last in his attic. It was low with a lumpy flock mattress and a bunch of iron grapes at the head. Coral untied the boy's arms from her neck and placed him in it. The other bed was occupied by Paula. A pair of glasses with Elastoplast over one lens lay folded on the floor and a hen's head lay beside her on the pillow watching them with a flickering eye while Paula breathed heavily through her open mouth. A wing was folded over the sheet.

'Paula, I've told you not to take Valerie to bed,' said Coral, taking the hen.

'Why not?'

'You might lay on her in your sleep.'

'Or vice versa,' said Dennis.

Downstairs she sat stroking the brown feathers while he told her of the meeting. He watched a watery globe roll down her cheek and burst on the patient hen. Can she still have some pride, he marvelled.

'What about the television?' she said. 'We'll never get another if they turn us out. We haven't got a licence.'

'But they can't turn you out! This is your home, don't you see.'

'The Authorities can do anything.'

'That's where you people are wrong,' he almost squeaked. 'You think that there's this omnipotent body called the Authorities against whom you are powerless. There are no Authorities!'

Coral only smiled because she knew better.

'Fight for your rights, woman! This is your slum and you and your children are entitled to stay in it.'

'What shall we do?'

'Absolutely nothing. I think you are going to receive a visit from Stella Oates tomorrow. She's the most dangerous but you are in no way obliged to talk to her. Don't let her in and don't let her near the children. I must go.' He stood up and Coral came with him to the door.

'I should have offered you a cup of tea.'

'Nonsense. Anyway I had some just before I came out. Here, buy the children something.'

'Thank you very much.'

He looked round at the gate and saw the hen turn and go into the house and the door close behind her.

Halfway home Stella overtook him in her car and stopped.

'Well, well, the social conscience of Filston himself. Hop in.'

'No.'

'Please yourself.' She wound up the window on his hand and he danced with pain on the pavement as she started the engine. She drove a few yards as he ran along beside her dragged into the side of the car, then suddenly wound down the window and accelerated so that he fell backwards on the pavement, hitting his head on a stone wall. He was seen staggering to his feet and it was reported to Joan that he had been drunk and incapable.

* * *

Coral crumpled the final notice from the Electricity Board, went upstairs and from her bedroom window saw Stella Oates, picking her way past the postman down the path to the back door. She ran downstairs to lock it, filled a cup with washing-up water, ran upstairs, tripped and spilled it, ran downstairs and refilled the cup, ran up again and deposited it in Stella's upturned face. She fled, her little mouth distended, gasping bubbles, clawing at her eyes with white hands.

She had once deprived a vicar of his living and, as a girl, had a captain reduced to the ranks and so she was not too disheartened as she drove to the police station to report the assault. A more recent success was the removal of a colony of gipsies from the camping site of generations: as they had plodded up the road in a heavy mist a coach had run into the back, smashing two caravans, three men and a horse.

* * *

'Please let me go to school,' begged Paula, torn between fear of the Attendance Officer and Miss Jigger.

'They shan't get their hands on you,' said Coral, hugging her until she thought her glasses would crack again. 'I know what they say about me in this village. I spend half an hour in front of the mirror choosing which rag to wear and stuffing paper in my shoes to make them stay

31

on and then they say: "Look at her, dirty slut, skirt thrown on any old how, slopping along in them shoes." As if I care what those drab toads think. You won't be going back to that school, they're hardly the class of person for you to mix with. Hurry up and find some shoes, we've got to get out of here.'

Coral loaded the baby and Ralph into the high black pram and locked the back door. Unerringly like a vulture she pushed the pram up and down hills between hedges as the sun grew hotter and burned through the holes in her black dress and made a burning glass of Paula's lens. She pulled handfuls of hawthorn leaves and stuffed them into her mouth without breaking the relentless rhythm of the wheels. The road degenerated into muddy furrows filled with brown and yellow puddles, a silo burned sullenly at the edge of a field of cabbages like a blue wheel and the pram rattled over lumps of lime. They were approaching a farm. As they passed the broken cobwebbed windows they saw beyond dangling rubber tubes the gaunt black-and-white hips of a cow. A fly walking on the baby's eye woke him and they stopped by the roadside while Coral fed him and the children looked for food in the hedge. Coral sat back against the twigs with closed eyes while her son dangled a bunch of elderberries at her closed lips.

They passed the farmhouse where rhubarb rampaged in the garden and red runner beans flowered on the strings and redcurrants cascaded on to soft green leaves whose scent brushed off on their fingers. In ten minutes they had filled the bottom of the pram and were on their way, leaving stripped bushes and dangling pods, while the dog barked and barked on the end of his chain.

They came round a sharp corner and there at the foot of a hill was a lorry smashed into a wall and bottles of cider and beer lying in pools of shattered glass around it in the road. They swooped down, and deciding that it couldn't be blood on some of the bottles, started loading them into the pram. Hopfields loomed behind them and the smell of malt rose from the glinting brown glass in the dust. Coral stood in the road and opened a bottle and let the cider gurgle down her throat. A grasshopper and a far mowing machine buzzed and a cracked bottle fell apart. She lifted the cider to her mouth again and again until the bottle was empty, and sank down into the roadside grass with her head under the hedge, looking up until chalky leaves, thorns and bits of petal fused and she lay asleep with her mouth open and the pram abandoned in a sea of burning glass.

A bicycle came grinding down the hill with both brakes on, spraying chalk dust on the powder-blue sky. The rider dismounted and walked down the road with glass cracking under his feet. Two children were slumped in the crushed cab of the lorry, a baby rolled on hot bottles in a pram in the middle of the road and a woman sprawled under the hedge. Coral woke with a great blue chin and helmet stuck in her face; a hand with a glinting steel band gripped her shoulder as he heaved himself into the grass beside her and hooked a bottle with his foot. She staggered to move the baby into the shade and tried to open the cab door but she could hardly lift her head for the pain in her skull and stood tapping on the glass with a stone watching her children huddled in their dissolute sleep.

The hot beer, twice as potent in the sun, foamed

through his teeth and his face shone red above his white throat and arms, his helmet rested on a sagging bunch of nettles, and he lay back, a boy policeman who would never be promoted, crushing an insect on his meaty lip without taking his eyes off her as she walked back to him.

'I'll report you to the Authorities,' she cried, tearing at silver buttons as a relentless knee pushed her back against the hedge.

'I am the Authorities.'

From her bed of thorns she watched him mount his bicycle and toil up the hill, a fading rose pinned to his receding hip. As she reached the lorry the door opened and a white-faced stained Paula fell into her arms and had to be carried to the pram. Ralph climbed down after them and, trailing after the pram with a bottle, sang the same song over and over in a high-pitched voice. She threw him across the pram and told Paula to put her hand across his mouth when they passed the farmhouse but now and then a note burst through her dusty fingers and hung like a bleat in the brazen afternoon, but he had fallen asleep again when they plodded up the lane in time to see Stella Oates, basket on arm, emerge from their gate, climb into her car and drive away towards the police station where she was told her assailant had received a stern warning, and was advised to let the matter rest.

Chapter Seven

'What's all that noise in the playground?'

'They're stoning Paula Fairbrother.'

'Ring the bell then, Miss Jigger, Nurse is coming this morning.'

As Nurse's car drew into the playground the children filed into the classroom. Paula, who had returned to school that morning accompanied by the Attendance Officer, stood red-eyed at the end of the queue and from time to time the boy in front kicked her without turning round.

'If you can't stand still and wait your turn you'd better go to the head of the queue,' said Miss Jigger, pulling her up like a fish on a hook.

Nurse combed her hair with a medicated comb and something jumped on to her white sleeve.

'Nails? Disgraceful, yes. Go and wait over there, dear.'

Paula waited on a wooden chair while the rest of the school filed past and were acquitted. The chair was hard and her throat stiff with trying not to cry. Now only she, Miss Jigger and Nurse were left. A smell of mince and gymshoes hung about the little cloakroom. She waited, heart thumping, wrists twisting in shrunk sleeves, and thought she felt something walking in her head as the wire shoe racks blurred like the squares on the page of a teary sum book and the two women whispered behind their great white hips.

'Come on Pauline, time for your haircut,' said Nurse, turning round. Paula held on to the pegs. Nurse spread a clean newspaper on the floor.

'Come along,' said Miss Jigger, 'you've already disgraced the school enough.'

'The first case in six years,' Nurse comforted her.

'Never mind that,' said Miss Jigger pulling at Paula's arm. Paula landed a kick in the vast skirt.

'Well, if the mountain won't come to Mohammed ...' Nurse dipped Miss Jigger's pinking shears into the disinfectant and advanced, snipping air. She inserted a blade and wrenched and chopped at the hair while Paula screamed and kicked in Miss Jigger's arms and a pyramid of faces swayed in the door. In the face of so much malevolence Paula collapsed and had to be supported by Miss Jigger as pieces of the pale hair which used to tangle in the frames of her glasses, dribble a trail of dry powder paint across her drab paintings and sweep on to the wings of a loved hen as her mother brushed it at night, fell on to the floor.

'Back, back,' shouted the girls in front, pushing backwards until the whole class crashed in a heap on the nature table. The wasps' nest was crushed and dead wasps rolled about on the floor, the beans in blotting paper were smashed, the old belt identified by Miss Jigger as a cast-off adder skin was lost. Miss Jigger heard nothing.

Back in the classroom Miss Jigger could not control outbreaks of scratching, by late afternoon some children had gouged deep red marks on their arms and legs that stood out like angry bites, but although Paula Fairbrother had fled like a maddened sheep from the shears Miss Jigger was in a benevolent mood, and after playtime, when she helped Nurse turn a skipping rope, even comforted the little boy who was sobbing hysterically because he thought they had cut off Paula Fairbrother's head, and explained that the blood was from a superficial neck wound. She decided to turn it into a history lesson.

'In the olden days,' she began, 'strange as it may seem to us in these days of the welfare state, the barbers were also the doctors and it was common practice to let a little blood for reasons of health ... ' but he wouldn't stop and had to be banished to the playground and that night woke the street with his screams. Miss Jigger, tossing in her rented bed with a plethora of cream on her face and her transistor buzzing under the sheet, heard nothing but the seconds of her life ticking away.

*　　*　　*

Joan watched the hateful hand pick a blister of paint from the gate she had painted. 'Really, Mrs Oates, I don't see what it has to do with you. I think you're running a personal vendetta against someone who can't defend herself and I reserve the right to employ whom I please.'

'Why can't she defend herself? She's got a tongue in her head, hasn't she? Your husband seemed very anxious to impress her intelligence on us the other night.'

'Good morning, Mrs Oates.'

Brave words, but Joan was trembling as she closed the

door and went through to the kitchen where Clare had been set the task of snipping gooseberries for a fool. Stella's words acted as manure on the doubts which had sprung up and now were threatening to choke her. She watched an idle brown leg swing over spilled gooseberries that would be trodden unless she picked them up herself and left the room before her voice turned into a reproach, allowing herself to slam the door slightly. She feared Clare would bring up the subject of the secretarial college in which she had been entered against her will when her parents had been advised that there was little point in her staying on at school, and she shut her bedroom door and lay down on the bed.

Dennis's hat slid across an unfamiliarly shiny hallstand when he came home. Some melancholy roses drooped in a sparkling glass on the kitchen table which had been scrubbed.

'I'm exhausted,' said Joan, 'Coral insisted on doing the whole house from top to toe.

'Dennis, why are you getting so involved with her?' she asked, although she had intended to wait until after the meal and place an arm around his neck.

'As her employer I –'

'I'm her employer.'

'I feel I owe her something more than money. She has no one to look after her interests and it isn't easy for a woman on her own. And I respect her because she has the courage to be herself.'

'At what cost to others?'

She heard the crash of drawers and tinkle of glass upstairs and quailed at the thought of another evening with Clare.

'You don't have to go out tonight, do you?'

'Would you like to come out for a drink later?'

'Just what I need.'

'Good. Perhaps I'd better just slip along to see Bill Smith about Saturday's match first.'

* * *

Dried soap bubbles on the floor and the cool smell of ironed clothes stopped Dennis on the threshold as he shut the door. Coral was sitting at the kitchen table and the baby, Stephen, sat on her knee which was muddy from kneeling, with drops of milk like china beads on his face, lapping cereal from a spoon, and behind them a bunch of blue scabious stood on the windowsill against the red sky. She led him from room to room and everywhere tatty tablecloths and drooping mats and worn linoleum had gone leaving bare furniture and wooden floors with wet patches still sinking into the splinters. Downstairs as she poured the stolen cider he exclaimed, 'It must be telepathy. You've had the same idea as me. We must stop fighting them and try to join them.'

'I see you have defected to the other side. Well I suppose I should have expected it.'

'Nonsense. A village ought to be a unit so we must bow to the will of the majority – that's why I'm doing all this work on the Parish Council. I'm sure if you were just to make the first move – people are quite nice really if you give them a chance. Think how much nicer it will be to walk through the village without fear of a stone. For the childrens' sake, Coral. Look, there's a fête tomorrow, why don't you come?'

She burst into tears.

'What's the matter, Coral? What have I said?'

'I've lived here all my life and you come here telling me about a fête!'

'Say you'll come, Coral, promise?' he pleaded, looking at his watch. She still looked unconvinced as he grasped her shoulder and ran out. In fact she smashed his glass in the sink at the prospect of another lonely evening.

* * *

The King's Arms had three doors marked PUBLIC, SALOON and SNUG, which all led into one vast room where red and blue plastic flowers bloomed in gilt-speckled vases on little scrolled shelves against the embossed flock wallpaper. A row of comical beer mugs leered above the hanging glasses, which sparkled only because the light shone on them. Stippled laminate chairs and tables, each with its metal ashtray on a central beermat, receded from the light in clumsy clusters to the comparative shadow of the walls. Four stools surrounded the oval bar in which the sullen landlord and his wife patrolled under a yellow light: they were so high that ladies had to be hoisted up and then sit hunched forward on to the bar with a black triangle between the knees and the stretched skirt, or with feet twisted round the metal legs so that, leaning backwards to laugh at a story, or extending a cigarette between clamped red lips, they overbalanced and came crashing down with wrenched ankles still attached to the stool.

'...walking by the riverside, the rustle of the little wild things...'

The man to whom she was talking, whose leg had been bitten to the bone in a badger hunt, shifted his cast and said nothing.

'Going to the fête tomorrow?' he asked.

'Should be,' said Joan. 'Dennis is one of the organizers.'

'Did you hear of that fellow on Filston Common that shot himself?' asked the landlord leaning across the bar and speaking for the first time that evening.

'Yes, shot himself.'

'My father shot himself,' said Dennis.

'Go on.'

'Yes. It's a silly story but tragic for us as well as him. As a boy my father lost six front teeth when he fell off the back of a cart he was hanging on to and it made him very self-conscious, and he was teased a lot at school, so much so that he stole some money from another boy, ran away and was brought back and expelled. He was always very strict about us children's teeth and we never visited the dentist and as far as I remember never needed to. Had a thing called toothbrush drill every night and morning, which meant we had to march to the bathroom, present toothbrushes, clean our teeth and march downstairs again for inspection. There were various penalties and awards and an annual shield which was hung in the bathroom and had a special place for the winner's toothbrush. Anyway, one summer when I was about twelve my father's younger brother, who was always a bit of a waster and who had just qualified as a dentist, returned from Australia. My father called us into the sitting-room and said to my uncle, "Take a look at these children's teeth, Mac." My uncle looked into each mouth, then shook his head gravely. "I'm sorry, Bill," he said, "but all these children are going to lose their teeth before they're twenty." My father went upstairs and shot himself.'

'Did you lose your teeth?'

'Of course not, it was only a joke.'

He stopped talking and looked at Joan who was running her finger round the rim of her glass which emitted a high buzz.

'Coral says every time you do that a sailor dies,' he told her and she snatched her hand off the glass.

Punctually the landlord called 'time' and dipped the glasses into the scummy water and pulled them out gleaming.

As Dennis and Joan strolled through the village afterwards, they saw a fork had been thrust into the baked weeds of Coral's front garden and a worm slid past something white in the upturned earth. A piece of paper was stuck on to one prong. Dennis pulled it off and read: YOUR TIME IS RUNNING OUT, in tiny blue writing.

'Stella!'

'But she hasn't disguised her writing! Doesn't she fear prosecution?'

'She has no cause to in this village.'

Joan folded the note and put it in her handbag and they walked on. They crossed a fence into a field of dark grass and sorrel and came to a narrow stone bridge. In early summer this part of the river was clogged with marsh marigolds but now slimy green stems and weeds had caught a passing stick which lay across the water trailing a swarm of minnows in a net of scum. At last with a shoeful of mud Dennis managed to dislodge the stick and disperse the muddy froth.

'We could trace the river from its source one day,' he said excitedly.

'Or look at the map when we get home.' Joan pulled a marsh marigold leaf. 'Coral calls them water bubbles,' she said, not realizing that henceforward her husband would always use that name. They walked on through the fields, and could be seen from the village striding about the moonlit hillside in identical anoraks.

*　　*　　*

Clare was waiting white-faced and half asleep in an armchair.

'What about a cup of – my God, Joan, I think I've got a flea.'

Joan and Clare came over to look at an insect sitting on his arm.

'Look, you can see his little legs,' said Joan.

Clare put out a pink thumb and squashed the flea against her father's arm.

Chapter Eight

Newcomers to the village, and Dennis was no exception, were often active on the issue of street lighting, but eventually the general apathy, despite periodic alarms of men with sacks and knives, led them to realize that the village preferred darkness. Now Dennis had thrown himself into the preparations for the fête. That morning while the mist still rose from the river he called on Coral and got her out of bed to persuade her to go to the fête as the first step in her rehabilitation. Standing on the step in a torn nightdress above her knees, she agreed.

Trestle tables were dragged out of the village hall into the Recreation Ground and flags strung across the navy-blue sky and hauled down again that afternoon as it began to rain. People crowded into the hall where old Coronation bunting and silver twigs hid piles of refuse from many jumble sales.

A little bald boy sold them tickets at the door and Coral with the children clinging pushed in among the steaming hostile coats. Old Mrs Fairbrother, crossing the hall to avoid her granddaughter, came upon her husband sorting through a pile of old clothes until he found a loved cap she had given away years ago. People who took off their wet coats risked having to buy them back at a Scout jumble sale three weeks later, or meeting others wearing them in the street. The greasy pole had been set up between two chairs, both of which broke when a boy placed his foot on it, and a group of men were tossing a pitchfork at a sack of hay. The rope from which it should have been suspended had been abandoned in the rain, so the sack was held up by two men who ducked when they saw the pitchfork coming and it smashed through a window at the back of the hall and on to the roof of the car of the mystery celebrity, who was to judge the baby competition.

For the first time Coral bought her children a glass of orange squash at the refreshment stall and bought herself a cup of tea. A hideous brown spider crack blotched the side of the cup.

'Excuse me, this cup's cracked.'

'Excuse me, you're a pauper and a pariah.'

'I could have taken it from anyone but her,' the woman told another when the children had been hustled from the stall.

'There's years of wear in that cup,' she replied.

It was a joyless afternoon; people lingered just to see the competition. Coral left Paula and Ralph in the alien crowd and walked with burning face and her eyes fixed on her baby through the path cleared by drab skirts drawing away and took her place with the thirteen women who stood with their groomed babies on the stage. Ten withdrew. The celebrity, who remained a mystery, walked up and down twice to limited applause while the vicar failed to catch his eye.

'Babies, ladies and gentlemen, in view of the small number of entries I feel it would be unfair to award three prizes as advertised. Besides which it would be almost impossible to choose. The general standard is very high and it is with great difficulty, and no hesitation that I choose Number Four, Mrs ... ?'

'Coral Fairbrother.'

'You can't have her, she's mental,' came a shout from the back of the hall and 'Mental', 'Mental', came from all sides and Coral, shielding the baby, fled backstage, pursued by old annuals, shoes and a cricket ball. The vicar fell, stunned by a plimsoll and the battery stopped as a last aluminium teapot clattered on to the stage beside him.

Coral left by a back window with her prizewinning baby and saw Ralph and Paula thudding down the street flat-footedly with flying shoelaces.

Later, under cover of darkness, the vicar came round with the £10 prize money. He had picked up the plimsoll that struck him and rooted round for one that matched. Now, on one grey and one khaki foot, he padded down the path and bumped into Dennis who found the door locked against him. He shouted at the window until she appeared.

'Why didn't you leave me alone in my squalor?' she cried through the glass.

'Were you happy?' he shouted.

'No, but I didn't think I had any right to be.'

He turned away and went home.

Chapter Nine

An old Brownie named Brown Owl sat on a mossy log surrounded by her picnicking pack, looked at her watch and hoped for a drop of rain or the threat of thunder so that they could leave the uneasy little wood far above Filston. A Brownie found a broken shoe, picked it up and poured a stream of dirty water down her tunic and screamed. It seemed to Brown Owl that silence had closed on other screams in this wood. She suggested they go and find a sunny field but the Brownies sprawled about the wood didn't answer. Years of fallen leaves lay under the dark yew trees. Now and then the shouting suddenly stopped and the Brownies stared at each other until the heavy silence was broken by a giggle or the gurgle of a bottle. Brown Owl, applying an Elastoplast or wrongly identifying deadly nightshade, was always aware of the trees beyond. Then she made up her mind; she had seen a nylon stocking hanging from a tree. Then she reeled over among the screams – she had been expecting a man.

A wild brown woman in scarlet rags crashed through the wood, cracking branches and screaming. Brownies scattered as flying hair whipped the unconscious face of Brown Owl and a sandwich was torn from her fingers. Individual jellies in paper cases, eggs, rolls, were scraped up with leaves and beech-mast and thrown into a sack and then the woman was away through the trees, leaving behind wailing and lemonade leaking into the leaves.

* * *

'Is this the woman who attacked you, Miss Owl?'

She had broken from her captors, and stood panting down on Brown Owl's chair.

'Can you recognize her?'

Brown Owl knew that in her dreams she would feel brown fingers at her throat, unable to cry out in the suffocating wood.

'No! That's the one!' she cried, pointing to a neat little person passing the window with a basket of eggs.

'Come now, Miss Owl, that's our Mrs Oates.'

'That is she,' she insisted, and persisted until she was led out trailing a broken sandal strap.

Chapter Ten

The wailing had gone on all night until the children fell asleep exhausted but at 2 a.m. Coral got out of bed to tie a belt tightly round her empty stomach. At seven the baby woke again and woke the others so she put him in the pram and they trailed along the empty street to Mrs Fairbrother's house to beg for food.

'A borrower nor a lender be,' said the old woman out of an unfamiliar toothless mouth. Paula pushed past her and ran into the kitchen knocking things over as she grabbed a tin of fruit, a jelly and a packet of biscuits; a sheep's head stared clammily from a plate as slices of bread fell one by one into a pool of milk and were devoured by a fox terrier. She ran out again past her grandmother who gathered the nightdress she wore over her clothes up above her knobbly old feet in a shrill dance of rage on the step.

*　　*　　*

Mr Thompkin, on his way to early service, wondered why that dirty family was eating raw jelly in the road at twenty past seven in the morning but was pleasantly surprised to see old Mrs Fairbrother up and about.

'Hang on, I'll walk along with you,' she called and slipped off her nightdress behind the half-closed door, placed a hat on her head, grabbed a set of teeth and joined him as the bell began its final peal.

Absent-mindedly chewing her wafer, she hurried back to her pew and by the time she was on the church path her ankles were kicking each other in her eagerness to get home. She harnessed Trixie and waited impatiently at the bus stop outside a garden of wet dahlias in the morning mist with a drop at the end of her nose, and was knocking with a gnarled fist on the pet-shop window when the young man arrived to open the shop.

'I've come to sell this dog.'

'I'm afraid we don't buy.' He unlocked the door without looking at her and she followed him into the smell of mice and sawdust. He sensed that a claw was about to be laid on his arm and moved to the back of the shop.

'Perhaps you could make an exception just for once?' She prodded at a sad pyramid of tortoises.

Above the sprays of millet, slabs of quivering horse-meat and fish fluttering in the dim tanks that lined the walls, hung a grey-and-pink parrot in a cage.

'I'll take him in exchange,' she said, taking it for some sort of pigeon and intending to eat it when she got home and hang a geranium in the cage.

'I'm afraid not, madam. That's a valuable parrot.'

'Fair exchange is no robbery,' she answered, putting Trixie on the counter, where she began to tear at a lump of meat. He looked with distaste at the parrot hunched in its musty cage and then at the alert little dog.

'I shouldn't really,' he said, 'that's a very valuable bird.'

'The dog and ten shillings, I can't say fairer than that.'

'Done.'

'You'll have to give me the cage as well and I'll take some seeds and one of those cuttlefishes.'

When she got home, after a glass of stout, she uncovered the cage and poked the piece of cuttlefish through the bars.

'Pecky, pecky,' coaxed Mrs Fairbrother.

'Why don't you shut your stupid mouth?' replied the parrot.

Chapter Eleven

There were certain fields, where the cows were vicious or sheep panicked, that Coral usually avoided, but this morning the Fairbrothers were filling a bag with blue damsons from three trees which were separated from the rest of the field by one strand of wire, behind which stood a great white bull.

The first warning shot sent two crows flapping out of a pine tree; the second sent the bull bellowing round the field with a splash of blood on his white shoulder.

'Run for it!'

They ran to the shelter of the ruined sty where the pram stood among piles of rotting sacks and cartridge cases.

'Is it the farmer, Mummy?'

'If it is he's within his rights to shoot us, we're on his land.'

Paula and Ralph were gibbering and crying.

'Oh shut up. Here, have a crab apple.' A bullet bounced on the asbestos roof. 'Paula, get in the pram. Ralph, lie between the wheels and hold on!'

She charged across the rough field pulling the pram over a trail of broken mole hills. She fell and the pram ran over her leg and dragged her to her feet. There wasn't time to negotiate the iron strips that bridged the stream.

'Keep your head up, Ralph.' She was hit in the leg as she plunged into the mud. A bullet fell into the stream and water rushed over Ralph's head as the pram tilted forward and his mother sank into the weeds; a crayfish was walking over the stones to his face, then he was jerked up and flung on to the grass with water pouring from his mouth and nose. Coral, with tears running down her face, was tying her cardigan round her muddy bloody leg.

*　　*　　*

'I think it's Thursday,' said Paula hovering on the edge of the bedroom where her mother lay with her leg wrapped in a strip of sheet.

'So?'

'Do you want me to go to the post office?'

'No.'

'What about the money?'

Coral placed a pillow over her face and when she removed it Paula had gone.

*　　*　　*

The iron stove had been lit for the first time that year at the Parish Council meeting and the four people seated round the table coughed and shuffled papers in the smoke. Stella Oates stood up.

'I expect you're wondering why I was so insistent that you attend this meeting. Well, I won't beat about the bush: Mr Gutteridge has something to tell us.'

She sat down dabbing at a smoky tear on her chamois-leather cheek. Mr Gutteridge took two pieces of paper from his pocket.

'This', he said, 'is my resignation. And this is the entry form, duly signed and sealed, for the best-kept-village competition. It is now two weeks after the closing date for entries. All I can say is I'm sorry. I've had a lot on my mind with my late wife's funeral etc., but that's no excuse of course.'

He pushed back his chair and walked down into the smoke. Someone called after him but they heard the door click.

'That's that, then,' said Stella. 'Now, besides electing a new member we've got to find some other excuse for getting rid of Coral Fairbrother. I may say that I had already put the machinery into motion but if I know anything about the working of local government nothing will be done.'

The others were still stupefied by Gutteridge's resignation.

'Why, Stella? There seems no need now.'

'These meetings are supposed to be public. Why does no one bother to attend?' said Dennis.

'She's got to go. She infects the whole village morally and probably physically.'

'Hear hear.'

'Let's get down to business, gentlemen.'

Stella picked up a glass of water but a film of coal dust had settled on the surface.

Afterwards, as they walked through the empty recreation ground past a W.I. poster advertising a talk by Stella Oates on the advantages of the factory system of farming, Dennis said to the man beside him:

'I wonder if Stella's hate for Coral Fairbrother doesn't stem from something personal? Wasn't there some scandal about her husband? It was before my time of course, but I seem to remember somebody telling me something of the sort.'

'Oh no, he –'

'My husband was as chaste the day he died as the day I married him,' snapped a voice behind them. Cold sweat leaped on Dennis's back and his foot missed the concrete step. Stella passed them and, sitting rigid in the blazing squares of the car windows, drove up towards the cold sunset shining on the stubble fields above them.

Chapter Twelve

The flocks of cyclists that flashed through the village all summer were less frequent and fewer fish with bloody throats lay on the banks of the river or in battered round jam-jars. From late July Dennis had watched with unease the reddening haws, the first yellow leaf to flatten on the road. Big blue cabbages, dahlias and chrysanthemums grew in the allotments, separated by wet grass paths from michaelmas daisies in neglected plots, and the white fluff of willow-herb drifted over everything. On his way home Dennis passed a giant striped marrow being wheeled to the church. After dinner he stood staring out at the garden.

'Dennis, dear, what's the matter?'

'It's nothing.'

'Won't you tell me?'

He turned to face her. 'It's this terrible vacuum.'

'I'll tell Clare to switch it off.'

'No, no, I mean this terrible vacuum inside me.'

'Look at those damned dahlias,' he said later. 'Another year gone. What's to become of us, Joan?'

'Become of us? Why nothing of course.'

All night Joan was aware of him tossing and scratching beside her and once woke to say, 'Why don't you go to her then?' and snatched the sheet round her when she found a great harvest moon leering through the window on an empty pillow. In the morning it was discovered that three gardens had been ravaged and broken dahlia heads and ripped red and yellow and purple petals were scattered over the road and turned to mud under the wheels of cars.

Joan had never felt so far from him as that day when she thought of him sitting inaccessibly in his office while she walked with the wind tugging at her skirt beside the river roaring at a flood depth of eight inches.

*　　　*　　　*

The dry wick sputtered, smoke swirled round the glass globe and the lamp went out. The pan round which she had been scraping the last chip fried with vinegar leaves clattered into the sink. Coral walked in the familiar dark to the foot of the stairs and listened until she heard three separate breathings in the quiet night. The day was over and there was nothing for her to do but lie in bed and think of lost opportunities and wait for sleep. She went back into the kitchen and a mouse ran across her foot as she groped for the biscuit tin and took out some of the money that had come from Australia and Joan Blake had changed for her. She put it back and crept upstairs to undress in the dark and get into the cold sheets.

In the morning she stood staring through the sheet of rain that fell past the back door to see what had kept Paula so long with the hens, and realized she had run off to school. A letter had come from the Authorities threatening prosecution and from this morning on Paula set out like a pale little martyr, returning at lunchtime to refuse the hard food that could not pass her knotted throat, learning nothing.

One Saturday morning Coral came downstairs to find her trying to fit a pig's head on to a horse in a farmyard jigsaw. A grisly scene erupting into grass and a horse-legged cloud and a smiling farmer upside down in a family of ducks was spread on the floor.

'Put on your glasses, dear,' said Coral and while she groped for the battered frames somebody knocked on the door. There was a thud on the ceiling followed by a silence, then screams. Coral rushed upstairs and found the baby lying on the floor.

'Ralph, Paula,' she called, 'Stephen's learned to crawl.'

The letter-box was rattling. She felt his silky skull; it wasn't fractured, then she sat on the bed until he had stopped crying and the letter-box was quiet. When she went downstairs a blue letter lay on the bristly mat.

'Children,' she said, coming into the kitchen. 'Your grandmother's dead.'

'What?'

It seemed she had died on a trip to New Zealand, but whether from heart-failure or from falling into a hot spring was not yet known.

Chapter Thirteen

'Snow! Snow! Snow!'

'You'll be in tears about it by nightfall.'

She was right. When night fell at four o'clock they were huddled, with their chilblained toes stuck out, like litters of pigs in front of the sodden clothes that hung round the wet wood fire whose only flame was orange lichen.

There was a knock on the back door; they sat staring at each other. The knocker knocked again and again and eventually she opened the door to find Dennis Blake gibbering like a cod in the snow.

'Have they gone?'

'Yes – I suppose they're in Austria by now, cruising down the nursery slopes.'

'Close the door, the snow's coming in. I'm putting the children to bed.'

'Who'd like a piece of chocolate to take up to bed? Let me see, where did I put it?'

He started patting his snowy pockets.

'Oh dear, I must have forgotten to pick it up. I know I left it ready on the hall table,' he said, sitting down and unbuttoning his coat, but after watching them hobble back to the fire on bandaged feet he had to get up and go out again into the snow. When he came back they were in bed and Coral was holding a newspaper in front of the fire which had started to blaze. He gave her the chocolate to take up and poured them both a drink.

'What a lovely surprise,' she said, raising the glass to her ashen lips, and swayed almost into the fire. He caught her and she fell back in her chair and he saw a lump bulging under a strip of sheet round her leg.

'What's that?'

'What?'

'On your leg?'

'It's where they shot me.'

'But that was weeks ago.'

'I got the bullet out but it doesn't seem to heal.'

'Let me have a look.'

But the glass fell from her hand and shattered gently on the floor.

She woke to find a dark shape against the oil lamp in her room. The burning and the dock leaves had gone from her leg and in their place was a clean white handkerchief.

'Still here?'

'As long as you need me.'

'Where did you live before you came here?' she said, to end a silence.

'Shall I tell you the story of my life?' he asked, stroking her forehead, not seeing in the dark that she had gone back to sleep.

'The first important event of my life was on an afternoon when the assembly hall was full of red roses and the curtain had risen on the fourth act of *Macbeth*. "What, you egg!" I cried and smote him through the heart with my wooden sword. For five minutes the prompter hissed at us while I stood staring at the blood leaking through his tunic until they brought down the curtain and carried him off. I had to be treated for shock so I put the thermometer against the radiator when Sister went out of the room. There was another boy there, I remember, who had got a cricket ball on the ear, and he said, "I thought you were supposed to be in the play this afternoon."

'"I was," I said, "but I've just killed Skelton with my wooden sword."

'"Oh very funny, Blake," he said and turned his swollen ear to the wall.

'I lay there making little flicks in the air with my wrist, feeling again the thrust and the sinking, and had to drop my head foolishly and burst into tears when I saw a policeman standing there in the doorway. I won't bore you with the details, suffice it to say I was acquitted after several weeks of hiding a grin under the corner of a sickroom blanket. I was asked to leave school of course, but granted a special dispensation to take School Certificate after school hours, and my prefect's badge was handed back at a small ceremony on the morning of Skelton's funeral. As I walked back down the drive that morning with my books I thought I felt a stone hit me on the cap but I didn't care – I was so happy. I just used to lie on my bed all day pretending to study and feeling Skelton sag on the end of my sword. For a time I used to find things like the chain taken off my bicycle or words chalked on our gate. I used to try to clean them off at first because they upset my mother, but if Skelton was at the point of my sword when I heard the chalk and running feet – too bad.

'Anyway after a bit we had to move away and it began

to wear off and I got terribly irritable. I used to have it all arranged, everyone in position, shout out, "What, you egg!" plunge my sword, and nothing would happen, either Skelton would fall grinning to the ground, a clumsy schoolboy in a tartan skirt, or else my sword would twitch on nothingness.

'I started going out for long walks at night round the district we'd moved to, it was winter by this time, and one night as I was coming round the corner past a pub, I saw a girl come out of a little terrace house and walk quickly into the fog. She disappeared but I could hear her shoes tapping along in front of me and I thought if I could get hold of her shoes by the heels and tip her out, pour her on to the pavement ...'

Coral had turned over in her sleep and he thought she hid her face to stop hearing him. When he saw she was asleep he tiptoed heavily downstairs and when he put his shoes on and crunched out into the snow his socks were full of splinters.

Light blazed from on the hill where the corrugated asbestos had fallen from the window of a battery and the whimpering of beakless hens came down across the white fields into the valley.

*　　*　　*

Before the morning snow had filled his footprints Stella Oates had picked her way along and was standing on the muddy doorstep like a praying mantis, with her hands round a thermos of soup.

'What do you want?'

'I thought you might need cheering up on this bitter

day so I've brought you some hot soup. How are the children?'

'None the better for your asking.'

'I do believe this is the worst winter I can remember,' said Stella, pivoting past into the kitchen.

'I'll put it here to keep warm,' she said putting the thermos on the cold stove.

A desperate damp coldness clung to furniture and folds of garments, a fungus of ice grew over the window so she did not see two children wrapped in a blanket staring from the corner until one of them started to cough. She took a step back.

'You should have that cough seen to.'

'Why don't you leave us alone? Why do you hate us so much?' Coral quavered, picking at the moss at the back of the sink.

'I don't know really. Perhaps it's because you're an outrage to public decency but I don't think so. You're just anathema to me.'

'You can't persecute me, it's against the law.'

'You're on the council's black list, you know.'

'What are you talking about? Black list!'

'Oh yes you are,' she trilled in a puff of frozen breath.

'Get out!' Coral came at her as if she would pick her up, bend her double, shove her into the open oven and slam the door. Stella snatched the thermos and shook it in front of her face.

'See this soup?' She tugged at the stopper. 'I'm pouring it on your filthy floor, look. And do you know what I'm going to do with your filthy floor? I'm going to rip it up board by board and batter down your diseased walls and steam roller your garden and any animals and children that happen to be in the way and build three bungalows in its place.'

She stood, waving the flask above her head, in a streaming puddle of soup the colour of the fleece that hugged her ankles, then threw it against the wall and marched out leaving the back door swinging open in a wind heavy with sleet.

Chapter Fourteen

Dennis set foot in the surgery for the first time, slipped on the mat and sat down heavily on a hop-stained lap. He felt himself sink two inches in the silence that greeted him, then she opened her knees and he fell through to the ground.

'I'm terribly sorry.'

'So you should be, mate.' Grunts of applause came from around the walls. He groped for a magazine and leaned against the wall, people started coughing and talking again. Twenty minutes later he raised his eyes over the page and saw her hobbling towards the inner door with a knee poking through a rent in the camel-coloured garment that hung round her legs. His turn came.

'Family enjoying their holiday?'

'Marvellous time, I suppose, I haven't heard yet.'

'Did you want to see me about anything in particular?'

'Yes, I seem to have picked up some chilblains somewhere.'

'Can't pick up chilblains, old chap. Still let's have a look – yes, chilblains all right. Ever had any before?' He bent his immaculate face over Dennis's feet. 'Of course you people will insist on wearing these ridiculous heels.'

'I hardly think — '

'No, of course not, I was thinking of something else. I'll give you some tablets.' He turned to his desk and, dipping his fountain pen into a square glass inkwell, began to write.

'I hope you won't take exception to what I'm going to say, I'm going to speak to you as a friend rather than your doctor for a minute. I do think you should be a bit more careful who you associate with. I mean – a magnificent creature and all that – but you don't want to get involved ... '

Dennis pulled the prescription from the bland finger and thumb.

'What do you mean, a friend? You hardly know me. How many of those people out there do you call friends?'

'Don't be silly, old chap. See you at the R.D.C.?'

'I'll see you in hell first.'

He thrust his feet into his shoes and stumbled into the waiting room, standing back to let a woman past, and as he stooped to tie his laces he heard voices through the plywood door:

'Sometimes I feel I can't go on, Doctor ... '

'Go on, Mrs Roe.'

*   *   *

He opened the door of the fridge and icy water fell on to his chilblained foot. He dropped some ice into his glass and took it through and stretched his legs out to the lonely glow of the fire and waited to feel the burning blood beat in his congested feet in time to the ticking of the clock.

* * *

On Twelfth Night morning Coral took down with relief the two Christmas cards she would no more have put away earlier than have brought hawthorn blossom into the house. She was counting the days until Joan's return when she would be able to go to work without gossip and sneers. Joan and Clare, with her thumb in plaster, came back a few days later but Coral did not see them for a week as Ralph and Paula had found a carton of groceries outside the village hall, awaiting distribution by the two ladies who bent sycophantic faces pinched with cold to the window of the car where Stella Oates graciously sat and had carried it away.

'Apparently she doesn't even draw her money from the post office any more.'

'Who doesn't?'

'Coral. How do they live, Dennis?'

He coughed. They were waiting for Clare to return from a college dance. The tinkling of a fire-engine in the hills before her heavy tread was heard at the door made them stiffen and stare at each other but it passed and the front door slammed.

'Think I'll be off then,' said Dennis, standing up so that his dressing-gown hung in gloomy folds round his legs. Clare came in for a few minutes with snow in her hair.

'Been sitting here boozing all night?' she asked

kindly. 'I've had a marvellous time. Good night, Mummy, good night, Daddy.'

She went out of the room leaving her parents feeling redundant. Dennis sat down again.

'Are we going out tomorrow evening?'

'You know we are. Why?'

'Just wondered.'

'It's nearly twelve – I'm going up.'

'What's wrong, Joan?'

'Nothing really.'

'But?'

'I do love Clare, Dennis, but I can't help thinking it can't be all I was created for. There must be something more.'

After a little silence Dennis got up and put his arm round her shoulders and said, 'There's me as well.'

'That's just what I mean. If I hadn't met you it would have been someone else.'

'Why don't you have a chat with the vicar?'

He got up and went to put the chain on the door.

'I wonder what Coral's doing?'

'Probably been asleep for hours, as we should have been.'

He rushed down and bounded back up the stairs with a bottle of whisky, two glasses and a soda siphon. Passing Clare's door he fired the siphon at it and the door opened.

'Ooh, a midnight feast! Can I come?'

Dennis held the door for her and bared his teeth at her back. She curled up on the end of their bed with her long feet tucked under her pale nightdress. Fifteen minutes later Dennis was asleep feeling as flat as the soda dribbling into the carpet from the siphon which Clare had kicked over with the toe of her slipper.

*　　　*　　　*

The last express flung through the station striking blue sparks and flashes from the frosty rails. The light in the station house went out. A slight fall of coal was followed by an indrawn shriek. Coral crouched in the intense blackness between two mounds of coal picking with numb fingers at the edge of a heap of coal glued together with frost. She realized she would have to hurry if she was not to freeze in that position; her shoulders were like razor blades pressed in on her by the cold and her knees were as stiff as frozen coal, her fingers slid on the frost, her knuckles knocked an overhanging rock and blood welled up and froze in the mesh of coal dust.

She straightened like a rusty penknife and lifted her sack, to find it only a quarter full. It dangled heavily from her hand and she put it down, then, taking a stiff black ear in each hand, swung it on to her back. The iron crust cut her legs and shocking soft snow filled her boots as she plunged into an old snow-drift while grasping for the gate. She found herself in the station garden picking a way among skeletal sprout stumps spiralling out to bar her way, with the sack banging on her back.

She blundered through a gap in the fence, and came out on the platform, giving a little sigh as the wind rose and moaned round the corrugated iron roofs and drove a powder of snow along the track. She staggered across the rails with the sack clasped in her arms, swayed for a moment on the top bar of the rimy stile and landed with a crackle of broken glass and frozen grass on the edge of the road. A light shone from the council houses on the hill above her, the only light in the sky. When it went out she was between two strands of rusty barbed wire with the black river running inches from her feet. As she struggled through her foot slipped and a stone splashed behind her. She was caught by her coat on the wire, she twisted and the fence sagged, a tree creaked above her and she remembered the treachery of elms, but this one could not betray her, she thought, with her knees grinding on a bed of stones. Then she remembered stolen fruit and broken branches and twisted on the wire beneath the moaning tree until her coat tore and she was free to go up the broken lane bent under her load and the cold.

'How did it go, Mum?' came a voice in the dark.

'Not too bad, better than usual.'

Chapter Fifteen

'Where's Clare? She's late,' said Dennis the following evening.

'At her driving lesson.'

'Oh yes, I forget. It's not like her, is it? I'm rather pleased.'

'If she keeps it up.'

'How's college going?'

'Oh, I don't know, she doesn't tell me. She seems a bit restless somehow. Still, it'll soon be her birthday. Think I'll have a bath.'

Dennis turned on the television and Joan went upstairs.

As she sat contentedly in the bath the soap leaped from her hand down the side of the bath. There was no more in the house and the bath was boxed in. She finished her bath, not letting herself think about it, but as she sprinkled Ajax on the faint rim she had left she was forced to face the empty shell soap-dish. Her knuckles rested on the bath's edge and would go no further. She spread a towel in the bath, gathered her pink robe around her, and stepped on to the towel and crouched with her eye to the space between the bath and steamy wall. A pale oblong shimmered in the darkness below. She rested on the edge of the bath and wondered whether to give up, but something drove her on and she opened the bathroom door quietly and ran down the soft stairs with her hand trembling like a moth on the white banister, past the sound of the television into the kitchen. She took the bread-knife and ran upstairs again. The blade scraped uselessly halfway down the wall, held at its full extent between her finger and thumb. She pulled it up again and mentally compared its length with the needles on which she had taught Clare to knit and remembered that they had been taken to support a sickly hyacinth. She went downstairs again and opened the back door and stepped with a feeling of exhilaration on to the frosty path whose stones burned her feet as she ran to the toolshed. A cold wind swirled up her sleeves as she fumbled at the wooden catch. Rusty tobacco leaves hanging from the ceiling creaked at her hair as she searched among heavy iron tools on the shelf until a blade gently serrated her finger. It was a hacksaw; she took it to the doorway and saw that the handle was too bulky and unscrewed the wing nut, pulled out the blade and laid the screw and handle neatly on the floor.

The blade was too short. She crept down again and bound the handle of a thin knife to the saw blade with a rubber band. This time she felt so close to triumph that she did not shut the bathroom door. The knife was wavering above the soap, was touching it, stabbing it, drawing it up to the rim; the blade and knife slipped and clattered to the floor. For a minute she knelt watching a drop of water rolling down a rose on the wallpaper, then was running down the path and was back panting again against the door with a screwdriver in her hand before the dew splashed on to the dew below. After unscrewing the screw she had tightened, it did not take long to draw away part of the surrounding board and put her face to the gap. Behind the iron leg of the bath she saw, festooned in dank weed, the soap, and saw that beneath the clean surface of their lives lurked unspeakable pockets of dirt. She hooked the soap and the saw and knife out with the bread-knife and put the soap under the hot tap in the sink, then screwed up the bath, sealing in its slime, wiped her footprints from the floor, washed the soap which was gritty and engrained until a mere sliver remained, which she put in the soap-dish, and went downstairs. She dismantled the blade and took it down to the shed where she placed it beside its handle and screws. Then she went in and sank into a chair in front of the television with her feet burning like ice, reliving the experience beside which the shelf of green chutney in the larder paled.

Chapter Sixteen

Old Mrs Fairbrother went into the grocer's and saw her husband standing mouthing in the middle of the floor, in slippers and a gaunt cardigan hanging from his sloping shoulders. There was a dry white stain round his mouth because, unable to make the shopkeeper understand, he had been given a tube of toothpaste on which he had been living the last four days until hunger had forced him out again. His great blue topless ear caught a familiar sound and he clutched at the counter and would have fallen but his knees would not bend.

'Give him a tin of beans,' said Mrs Fairbrother. 'On me.'

He stumbled and tried to turn round.

'Here,' she said, taking off her emerald scarf and tying it over his shaking head and pushing him towards the door, 'come on home, you stupid old faggot.'

Chapter Seventeen

Pea-sticks from the allotments were light and long but burned fast. Coral found the best firewood was logs sawn by the Forestry Commission and left beside the paths in the woods, but had several times suffered the disappointment of arriving at the site of a consignment to find tyre marks in the mud or slush and husks of bark where the pile had been. Hunger could be forgotten for a bit when they had twigs to dip into the fire and draw red patterns on the darkness.

Red feathery wheels stopped at the gate and footsteps came to the back door, went away again, returned, retreated and the wheels drove away. Coral opened the door and a pile of logs fell in; she did not know who they were from. Perhaps it was one of the children's fathers.

White wood and the smell of resin lit the dark kitchen as the logs rolled in.

'Pile it in the shed, Paula. We won't be using it.'

'It's too dark.'

'I suppose it can wait till morning then.' She closed the door on it and went back to find the fire almost cold and the air thick with damp washing.

* * *

At 8 a.m. on her nineteenth birthday Clare crossed to the window, in a drift of her favourite kippers frying, aware of her parents' anxious smiles behind her, and saw a little Mini standing in the road, a powder of snow already on its roof. Joan's only disappointment was that she drove off and did not return until the kippers were ruined.

The 'L' plates were off in two weeks. On the morning of that day Dennis closed the gate behind him, light hurting his eyes, and saw down the road past the newspaper blown against the lamp-post like a heap of unmelted snow, Stella Oates's newly purple head like the first crocus in the bright wind, and fell in love with her for a second as she stood in the empty street with seagulls dirty as flints pecking the brown-and-white field above her.

At school he had engineered a friendship with a boy because with his round blue eyes and yellow hair, the whole tomato that bulged from his mouth made up the three primary colours. However, Stella was getting into her car with the swing of legs monotonous to those who knew her and, hands placed not too close together on the wheel, was driving to the station. Dennis wondered why she had got out of her car but, when he passed the spot where she had been standing, saw nothing and walked on, occasionally forced by a car into swathes of white frozen grass.

Although it was years since she had held a licence Joan knew she would not be stopped by the village policeman if she took the car out. She was expected for tea that afternoon and didn't want to go.

At midday she was sitting with a cup of coffee on her

knee, tapping cigarette ash in the saucer while insane Light Programme music glittered on the sideboard, sometimes drowned by the whine of the electric fire and a submerged waterfall booming in the immersion heater. The cigarette grew soggy, the daytime wind rattled the leaded pane. She went upstairs and dressed, and watched a cat on the wall from the window while she rubbed in handcream, unaware that it was secretion of the civet her chapped hands drank so greedily.

When she had passed the police house standing behind its low wall in the flat white garden with drooping dwarf cypresses in the two round beds and a broken blue telephone kiosk, Joan let the muscles in her legs relax and the car shot forward between ditches of cracked ice. She realized she would have to visit a garage somewhere to conceal her journey from her daughter and saw in her mind a hazy petrol station at a deserted road's edge, five miles away in the hills. A tractor's engine running as a man forked cabbages off the trailer and hurled them into a field was the only sound, the tractor smoke and his breath the only movement until she swung crookedly round the concrete strip of the forecourt behind which lumps of snow splashed from the branches to the floor of a rotten wood. A young man with red hair and white eyelashes put down his book and came out of the little hut parked on the corner of the forecourt and walked towards her in an immaculate white boiler suit.

'Two pints please,' said Joan in answer to the foot placed on the fender.

'I haven't seen you round here before,' he said, reaching for the nozzle. 'You're a stranger like myself.'

'Really, I should have thought you were indigenous to

your surroundings.' She paid him and said, her face soft in the dull interior of the car, 'Young man, you seem in no hurry to take your foot from my car.'

'You're in no hurry either, are you? You've got nothing to do, have you?'

She began to start the engine, but he stopped her.

'Would you like a cup of tea?' His lips were already slightly inflamed with cold; he put out a purple-stippled hand with oil in the cracks and opened the door and guided her over a patch of ice to his hut. Joan felt she was being kind in granting her time to this lonely young man. The walls were hung with road maps and a girl knelt on a calendar in the Home Counties clasping Scotland above her fading head. A baby stove clotted and rusted with grease stood on a table against the wall and there was an electric fire beside the chair where Joan sat down. The boy went out and returned with a full kettle splashing at the spout. There was no hiss from the hot plate when he dumped the wet kettle and Joan reached over and flicked on the switch with a gloved finger and sat back swinging her leg lightly to show that she was at an advantage but did not like to ask him to shut the door.

'Do you run this place on your own?'

'Only when my uncle's in hospital.'

'Oh dear, I'm sorry, is it serious?'

'It is for me, I'm supposed to be studying.'

'So you're a student. What are you reading?'

'*Tarzan the Invincible.*'

'Oh,' she said, a little bewildered, her eyes flickering round the room, over the open paperback without seeing it.

'I'm studying to be an engineer. I ought to be at college but I'm stuck here till Monday. I'm very grateful to you, you're the first person I've seen all day. To speak to, that is. Am I the first person you've spoken to?'

'Of course not,' she admitted.

He shut the door and made tea and stirred it with a stained spoon and poured it before it had infused, burning his hand and swearing, so that Joan concluded that he was a very honest boy because she would have pretended she hadn't and perhaps presented an injured paw to Dennis at bedtime. They sat in their lighted box at the edge of the road and occasionally lights flashed past but never stopped.

'Well, Mrs D. Blake, when may I visit you at "The Shambles", Filston?'

Her cup clattered into the saucer.

'How did you know?'

'I saw it in your handbag which you left in your unlocked car. You haven't got a licence, have you?'

She stood up and her cup rolled down her knee and broke in two pieces on the floor. Her foot crunched on the handle. He stretched his long arms across the door; Joan saw herself beating frailly on his white chest and a laughing fist catching her hands and holding them like a bunch of black eels and sat down again.

'I don't know what your purpose was in luring me here. If it's money you can have what I've got. All of it and I'll never tell anyone, I promise.'

'Three and sevenpence?' he sneered, making it sound as foul as his grimed nails which were tapping the maps and twisting a green drawing pin out of the wall. She turned to the window and wailed, 'Stop, stop', at the tail lights of a car. He laughed and was stepping aside when she rushed at him with the chair and succeeded in pinning his neck to the wall with the bar of the chair; he grabbed the legs and pushed, falling forward on his knees and tearing the cage from his head. He stood up with a dusty smudge on each white knee. Keep calm, she told herself.

'Those overalls aren't yours,' she screamed, 'they don't fit. You've killed him, haven't you?'

He threw the chair to the floor with one hand advanced, his great hands squirming at the ends of stiff arms.

'Please sit down, Mrs Blake,' he said. 'I'm sorry I looked in your bag.' He picked up the chair and patted the seat. 'Would you like another cup of tea? Or perhaps you just want to get out of here.' He indicated the door.

As she went out on trembling legs he touched her arm with a humble finger.

She turned and saw red cascade down his throat and down the weal left by the chair.

'If you could forget this we could start again.'

'Young man, I don't think you know what you're talking about,' she said walking quickly to the car. 'I feel sorry for you – you're obviously deranged, perhaps through no fault of your own. But if I want to indulge my pity there are the collection boxes in the church.'

She looked at the little dead jewelled watch on her wrist, a relic of more efficient days, and opened the car door.

'I'll come on Tuesday next week,' he said, closing the door. 'You'll have had time to think it over.'

It was quite dark but she did not think to switch on the lights.

Dennis rushed out to a meeting almost as soon as he came in and when he returned was too preoccupied with wondering whether there had been a feeble attempt to send him to Coventry to notice his wife's disturbance, and they sat glaring at a newspaper and a book, each wondering why the other did not ask what was the matter.

Chapter Eighteen

Cold gnawed like a cancer in the bone and the wind bored through the heads of three figures crouched in sacks round the fire that fell apart with the finality of the last log. The tallest stirred and the sacking shifted to show a long sunken-eyed baby against her knees. He began to cry and wouldn't stop so she rolled him on to the heap of blankets behind them and gave him a turnip top to suck. The only sound they heard through the white hours of the days and nights was the moaning of telegraph wires and spontaneous outbursts of tears. The thin hen Valerie, sole survivor of the flock, sat on her legs in a corner staring at the shreds of bark left from the delivery of logs and pecked at and abandoned a curled-up wood-louse. Nobody had been upstairs for a week. Coral had thrown hot ashes from the back door, beside which a pipe had exploded so that a solid spew of rusty ice hung from its lip, to make a path down the garden. There was not much to talk about since Coral had forbidden the relating of dreams, all of which were of food, and they recoiled with spasms of the stomach from the thin soup standing by the fireplace. Dennis had not appeared since the night he bandaged her leg.

However, this evening they heard shouts of laughter and looked out of the window to see the mobile chip shop had stuck in the snow and was sending frantic puffs of smoke from its revolving chimney and showers of ice from its wheels on to the crowd round it. A tractor was called and bumped it gently into a snow-drift where it overturned. The watchers in the cottage turned away as people suddenly stared up at the window. They went downstairs to wait but when an hour later the van was driven away there was a patch of yellow fat in the snow but no chips.

When a knock sounded on the door at 8 o'clock it could only be Dennis. He had to heave his knees on to the window-sill and sank six inches in the snow; the doors had swollen and stuck.

'Did you see the chip van overturn?' he asked, during a lull in the silence. 'I think you've got the perfect baby there,' he said, nodding at Stephen. 'Never cries, does he?'

'About once a week.'

'What do you feed him on?'

'Same as we have.'

Dennis felt her attitude to him was not that of beneficiary to potential benefactor.

'Got any of that cider left?'

'No.'

'I've come to ask you, yet again, to let me arrange for your electricity to be reconnected, and Joan wants you to know that your job's still open if you want it.'

The sleeve pulled back to reveal a wrist become bony as she pointed to the window.

'Go.'

'Look here, Coral, it can quite easily be arranged.'

'We don't need it. No council employee will set foot over this threshold so you needn't try. The woods are full of wood. Do you think I'd let my children freeze?'

Newspaper crackled in Stephen's round woollen knees.

'What about your pension then?'

'Why do you persist in calling it that? Anyway I don't want it.'

'Family Allowance then. It's nothing to be ashamed of. Joan and I will be drawing our pensions when I retire. I'll have it paid straight into the bank.'

'Do you expect me to go crawling through the slush to the filth at the post office? Well, do you?'

'Joan's worried about you.'

'Out.'

'Don't watch me then,' he pleaded, opening the catch and girding up his trousers. Cold rushed up his legs as he crouched on the sill and jumped. He heard the window close as he plucked his hands from the snow.

'Why didn't you let him reconnect the electricity?' asked Ralph.

'If he wanted to I couldn't stop him.'

*   *   *

Joan had polished herself into a corner of the kitchen.

'Well,' she said, kneeling there, 'did you convince her? Look at your shoes!' she said, leaping across the room at a mop. 'Well, that's that. It's obvious she won't be coming back so I'm engaging someone else. We've done our best.'

'Rather an odd thing happened on my way back. I thought I saw Stella with an architect in the lane outside Coral's.'

She mopped savagely round his feet. 'Take them off and put them outside the back door.'

'You're not interested are you? What's the matter with you lately? You take no interest at all in me any more.'

'What? How did you know he was an architect?'

'He seemed to have a tripod. It was dark. What's on your mind?'

'Tea.'

In the midst of eating Dennis suddenly laid down his knife and opened his mouth to speak but the telephone rang and Joan rushed to answer it. It was a wrong number. On her way back she stopped in front of the mirror and arranged a piece of hair.

'Who wants me?' shouted Dennis.

'Nobody.'

'What do you mean?'

'A wrong number.'

'What kept you so long then?'

'Nothing.'

'It was he, wasn't it?'

'Who?'

'You know who I mean.'

'What are you talking about?'

He went on eating. Joan scalded her mouth with some coffee.

'I'm not often here at this time, am I? In fact I'm more likely to be found at a meeting. I expect you said, "Ring me this evening, I'll be at home doing nothing. No, my husband won't be in, he'll be out somewhere helping someone or campaigning for amenities." Who is it, Gutteridge?'

'Dennis, please.' A laugh was chilled in her throat as he looked at her. He stood up and went into the hall.

'Come here.'

She came. He was standing by the telephone.

'Fetch the secateurs.'

'Not the secateurs.' She backed away.

'Do as I say.' He turned to the mirror and she was faced with an implacable back and eventually crept down to the shed and returned with the instrument dangling from her hand. She threw them at his feet and had fled up two stairs when an iron pincer gripped her cardigan and pulled her down.

'Cut the wire.'

His eyes were shining like cracked light bulbs. She took the secateurs and snipped at the curly white wire.

'They're blunt.'

'Cut.'

It was severed and the tip of a red artery bled at the end of the trailing wire.

'Let that be an end to it. Replace the secateurs.'

She stumbled out and swayed down the path to the shed.

*   *   *

'Daddy, what's the matter with the telephone?' Joan heard Clare ask when she came in.

'There's a power cut.'

'Oh. Well, it's jolly inconvenient, I'm expecting a call.'

She heard the electric kettle whistle and a cup placed on a saucer. Dennis's behaviour with the telephone had no bearing on her thoughts about Tuesday because before it had rung he had eaten without comment a slice of the cake she had made that afternoon and immediately she had felt fully justified in any action she might take.

* * *

On Tuesday morning Dennis looked out of the bedroom window into sunshine so bright that people in the street were silhouettes, and turned away from the memory of an identical morning when he had heard that his friend of the primary colours had been killed, and he had proposed to Joan. The sun lit the weave of tumbled striped sheets and the grain of the wardrobe swirling like granular ectoplasm across the door to a vertical rainbow at the edge of the mirror. Joan called from the kitchen with an edge of stainless steel in her voice.

'You'll miss the train,' she said after a rapid breakfast in which plates jumped about and his cup was suddenly empty. His gloves were packed in his pockets and the front door grazed his back as he was sent down the path with vestigial leather hands sprouting from his hips.

* * *

'... by no means satisfied. We'll be back. Meanwhile you'd better fill her up.'

A blocked gurgle.

'Get a move on. What's keeping him, constable?'

'Nothing's coming through, sir.'

There was a liquid agitation. The constable kicked

the pump, the boy grabbed his leg as it swung back again, and they fell against the pump. The front fell off and a trussed man with viscous bubbles at his nose and ears fell at their feet while petrol flooded round them from the fallen nozzle.

But there was no such news in the paper that Joan read as she lay in the bath, the reason for which she would not have admitted to herself. She was hovering at the mirror in her slip when she vibrated with the doorbell. She seized a black dress from its hanger and thrust her arms in the sleeves and her head inside. The zip stuck and she was captive. The bell rang again. The boy on the doorstep extended his finger towards the bell again, but the door was opened by a black bat flailing at him and he fled down the path and slammed the car door on its shrieks.

Chapter Nineteen

If the tiled roof where moss showed once more had been lifted like a stone that morning the grey creatures beneath it would have been seen shrunken from the winter and shrinking from the invading sun.

As it seemed warmer outside than in as the morning passed, the old pram was pushed painfully along the iron ruts to the gate. Their weak legs followed the swaying wheels down the lane and at the corner Coral managed to divert the pram on to a beaten mud path that led to the river. The river was full and carried mud and moss and clouds over its waterfall and churned them against a dam of froth and branches. Bare thorns scratched the sky, Coral heard their footsteps fill behind them as they crossed a sodden field.

Upstream on a bridge, looking down at the willows in the water, the wind blowing the long black skirt and the tweed flaps that stuck at right angles above the plus fours, stood two men. They were the vicar of Filston and Martin Oates, only son of Stella, allowed home for the week-end to occupy the room which had been preserved like a shrine since the days when he had plunged sodden with aspirin into a black sleep. The floor was as bare, the bed with its army blanket as damp, the photograph of Stella as huntswoman as central on the green wall.

Martin pointed to something in the direction of Coral's cottage with his stick.

'What's that?'

'I think it's a house, Martin.'

'No, over there, look.'

'A house, Martin.'

'No, I mean that bird. Oh, it's flown away.'

'Yes, it was a house martin.'

Martin slashed at the grass with his stick because no one ever answered his questions, and started to walk on.

'Perhaps we shouldn't go any further,' suggested the vicar tactfully pausing a foot away from the broken stone support of a long rotted millwheel where Maxwell Oates, Martin's father, had been found, with a mouthful of gudgeon, wedged against a fallen willow trunk after the river had overflowed its banks for three days.

'No, it's all right, I often come here, honestly.'

After staring into the brown water they turned back and surprised a boy holding frogspawn like a bunch of grapes over the stream. When he saw them he ran with water spurting round his head, to a black pram sunk to its axles in mud.

*　　*　　*

'Where did you go?' asked Stella across empty plates, rigid knives and forks and the spot of gravy on the cloth at Martin's place.

'Along the river,' he said nervously, fitting his knuckle into a dent in his forehead reputedly caused by the constant parking of his pram, by the girl who looked after him, under the dripping tin roof at the back of the King's Arms.

'I met the vicar and we ... ' he trailed off as a woman came in, took the plates and placed coffee on the sideboard.

'How far did you go?' she asked, pecking at her cup. She ate like a bird, and although Martin had surprised her in the larder with a beakful of bread, he was forced to make up with bags of boiled sweets which had turned the inside of his mouth to a sponge.

'As far as the old dam?'

'Yes.'

The rims of Martin's eyes turned as red as the dull bar of the electric fire. He pretended to cough and pulled out a great boyish handkerchief to wipe his eyes, and a splinter of boiled sweet pierced his eye.

'Really, Martin, I sent you away to school to overcome that sort of thing. Do pull yourself together.'

He trumpeted noisily into his handkerchief. Stella tinkled a little brass bell disguised as a lady. After a few minutes the woman who had served lunch stood sullenly before them drying red foaming hands on the green flowers of her apron.

'I think perhaps you'd better give Master Martin some aspirin and take him to bed.'

'No, Mrs Oates, I won't. Perhaps Master Martin's had too many aspirin in the past.'

She backed against the sideboard and closed a drawer behind her trapping her apron strings.

'You can take a week's notice in lieu of wages.'

'You ugly old bat, I'd have gone years ago if it hadn't

been for Martin. If he was mine he wouldn't be wearing those long stockings at his age.'

Martin writhed in his father's plus fours. She took a step forward; the cutlery drawer was wrenched out, a volley of knives, forks, spoons and meat carvers pierced her back and crashed to the floor; the sideboard doors flew open, a tantalus slid out and pale gold liquid streamed round the scattered silver. Martin leaped forward, slipped on a knife and sat back gasping with a toasting fork quivering in his knee.

'Get out.' Stella grasped her coffee cup so hard that the handle broke off and lay in her hand as bent and white as her little finger.

Mrs Leech led Martin into the kitchen.

'Sit down here,' she said, pushing him gently on to a wooden chair. 'Let's have a look.' She snatched at the toasting fork with a nervous hand, missed, and then plucked it out slowly and jerkily. 'Easy does it,' she said, prolonging the agony.

The rolled trouser revealed two white wells slowly filling with red. Mrs Leech snapped on an Elastoplast.

'Some of the lads are going stock-car racing this afternoon. Why don't you go along? My nephew's going. It would do you good to get out with some young people.'

Martin agreed and limped out to the garden and hid in the shed until Mrs Leech's nephew passed the dusty window, and Mrs Leech's voice had stopped shouting from the kitchen door. When the light rain that turned the dust on the window to mud increased and rattled on the roof, Martin slunk back to the house, re-entered by the front door and went up to his room. At three o'clock, with no means of telling the time, he was driven downstairs by hunger.

'Martin!' He froze at the larder door with his toes turned in, then resolutely directed them to the drawing-room where Stella sat. Martin bent his knees and sat.

'You gave me an idea this morning when you were telling me about your walk. Will you do something for me tonight? Can I trust you, Martin?'

'Implicitly, Mother,' he barked.

'This could mean a lot to me. I think I've found a way at last. I've been thinking about it for a long time but I'm afraid I've been very naughty and let precious time slip away.'

'What do you want me to do, Mother? It's not like you to beat about the bush.'

'No, it isn't. Well tonight, after midnight, I want you to go to Miss Coral Fairbrother's house and block up all the drains and drainpipes. Do you understand?'

'With what?'

'Old newspaper. All the pipes of the house and any drains you may find around that filthy shed in the garden. If you can't find enough newspaper there's a pile of parish magazines in my bookcase.'

As he stood up she said: 'Mrs Leech seems to have left us. I think I'll just have a lightly boiled egg for tea. We'll manage on our own, eh, Martin?' She patted the leather patch on his elbow.

At ten past twelve that night a dark figure pushed open the gate with difficulty and walked through the long grass to the back door. A drainpipe tore away from the wall with a rusty groan in his searching hand. He crouched and stuck his hand up its slimy mouth, suppressed a scream and forced himself to thrust the unskilfully crumpled parish magazines up as far as they would go.

An upstairs window was pushed up and a face floating on candlelight said, 'Who's there?'

'It's only me.'

'Who are you?'

'The Water Board, madam.'

'What on earth are you doing?'

'Just unblocking your drains.'

The window closed. The back door opened and for a second by the light of the candle they faced each other, each in a way contender for the title of village idiot. Martin smiled, then a sluice of cold water knocked him backwards.

*　　*　　*

'Martin!' She was standing at the stairhead in an old camel dressing-gown of her husband's, gathered up, to Martin's horror, around thin shanks in sheepskin slippers.

'Is it done?'

'Yes, Mother.'

'I've made you some cocoa in the kitchen. Just boil the kettle and add some water. Are all the drains blocked?'

'Yes.'

Four days later, the wind of Ludgate Circus blowing his trousers round his calves, Martin found Stella's letter to the sanitary inspector complaining of the persistent stench from drains and subsequent menace to health in his pocket and posted it.

* * *

'Good morning, madam. Do you mind if I take a look at your drains?'

'Why all this sudden interest in drains?'

Over his shoulder Coral could see a posse of red bicycles riding down the lane. Men in black uniforms swung their legs over and dismounted and converged behind the inspector. He began his inspection, watched by pale faces from the door. The first pipe yielded a clogged mass of paper, the second a feather, another two skeleton leaves. One of the men lifted the grating from each drain and replaced it with a disappointed look. Eventually they had to ride away.

Stella, entering a shop, saw them ride past and paused between a barrel of cabbages and a dustbin to watch them disappear, then went in and said quietly to the shopkeeper:

'I see the sanitary inspector has got round to doing something about those drains down the lane at last. Sometimes the smell's terrible as you go past – we even get it up at my house when the wind's in the wrong direction. Horrible, isn't it, to think of all those poison bacilli swarming around in those blocked drains and getting into our water supply?'

She straightened as feet sounded on the floor behind her.

'Any eggs, madam?' asked the shopkeeper loudly.

As she left Stella said, 'I wouldn't be surprised if a lot

of the undiagnosed illness in this village could be traced to those drains,' and walked out confident that she had placed virulent germs in a mind which was a breeding ground for imagined disease. The shopkeeper repeated the conversation to the next customer, attributing Stella's words to himself.

Chapter Twenty

Birds' brittle voices like the black twigs against the hyacinth sky twittered in Dennis's ears as he left the station. Energy boiled in his legs, but he did not break out of the formation of dark figures walking neatly at regular intervals down the road. Now and then a workman swooped past on a bicycle. A faint smell of pigs drifted from asbestos sheds in the field alongside. All colour had faded from the sky when he came out of his house and set out along the river and crossed an unknown fence. It was so quiet, but old hoofprints in the mud, briars of barbed wire curling from the elder trees, a rusty water tank, showed that someone had been there once. Wings fluttered in the dank bushes and a girl flung herself at him, throwing her arms round his waist as he stepped back in horror at the yellow teeth laughing from pale shrunken gums.

'Paula.'

She turned and waved with a purple arm stretching bare to the elbow from the sleeve of her coat. Ralph stopped a few feet away, his bloodless lips open and his hair like thistledown in the wind that rubbed dry branches together and made the willows creak above the darkening water. Dennis waited, fearing the children were alone, his hand clenched round a fence post while Paula danced around him. A shuffling sound was coming along the path. He bent and, looking along the tunnel of warped trees, saw a pair of men's short rubber boots dragged along by feet that never left the ground. He ran to meet her, Paula clinging and Ralph trailing. She walked unevenly on legs scaled with mud, Stephen on her hip.

'Let me take him.'

'He's heavy,' she said, tossing wild hair from her eyes. He prised Stephen from her hip and nearly dropped him he was so light.

'Has it been a bad winter?'

'Judge for yourself.' She waved a hand at the children waiting against the twisted elder like two more stunted plants in the mud, and started walking.

'Coral, there's a limit ...' he said desperately, walking backwards in front of her.

'Yours came pretty soon.'

'You can't blame me for this.' – Ralph and Paula and Stephen's head lolling like a stone on his shoulder.

There was no answer but the scrape of boots.

'It was hard for me too, Coral, knowing your circumstances, unable to help. Wondering if the roof was leaking, or the pipes had burst, or if you had enough to eat or if the children were ill, or you.'

'It wasn't far to come to ease your mind.'

'I couldn't come after the way you sent me out of the window. I might as well tell you, you know already, I loved you, Coral, and you just looked on me as a provider of food and money; I wanted you to need me for myself.'

'Oh we didn't need you. Cattle and sheep have to eat in winter. They throw down cabbages in the snow. The pipes did freeze but we had enough icicles to drink and when the pipes burst we all had a bath. I suppose now that spring's here you feel safe to emerge from under your stone. Well, you could have come before and it wouldn't have mattered – we have ways and means of surviving.'

*   *   *

Halfway up Station Road in a heap of black leaves, his rucksack suspended by its straps in the air above his shoulders, Martin was stooping to examine a pale blue-bell leaf pointing bleakly through the mould when a car horn blasted him face downward in a tangle of chestnut roots.

The door of a white Mini flew open, an arm in white pulled Martin to his knees.

'What are you trying to do? I could have killed you!'

'You could have killed me!' Martin rose and con-fronted Clare. 'Miss Blake, isn't it?'

A rattling on the tin bridge at the top of the road.

'My train,' mouthed Martin, helplessly watching the green segments pass.

'You look as though you're going to cry.'

'No, I'm not, it's just that I was late three times last week.' He stilled a quivering lip as the guard's van dis-appeared.

'Well don't just stand there,' Clare heard herself say to the back of the head with ears flushed by cold or em-barrassment, staring at the empty bridge. 'Get in the car and we'll try to catch it at Henton.'

*   *   *

'Look,' Martin said, holding the door, one foot poised to glide across the icy forecourt, 'I'm in London all week, but could I see you at the week-end?'

'Saturday evening.' She released him and he ran to the approaching train.

Henton, clenched in a high valley among wooded hills, was a village people didn't visit, where the river froze and glued birds to the rushes; while other villages were bright with crocuses, heaps of yellow snow bloomed in its barren gardens.

Clare drove slowly along the street, past the playground where a child already stood as permanent as the frozen drip at the mouth of the drinking tap, past the nailed-up windows of the cottage where a young teacher and his wife from London had lived and died within a year. A black pleated paper lamp-shade pricked so that the light shone through like stars lay half under a bulging old sack by the gate. Another sack lay where the village sagged into a field, with a nylon stocking beside it. The Henton air filtering through the closed car windows restrained Clare's foot on the accelerator and she looked from side to side, at sodden stalks and bare poplars pointing to the grey mist rolling down the valley. Half a mile from the village she passed, not long locked up and rusting already, a garage.

Chapter Twenty-one

Glued to the end of the red sofa, a coffee cup tinkling at his foot, Martin watched the door desperately while Joan's conversation assaulted his ears.

The door opened and Clare stood at the edge of the room, a curt 'hello' on her lips which were inflamed by a slight cold. When they left Joan found a wet patch on the sofa caused by a crushed bunch of daffodils Martin had been sitting on. Clare swung into the passenger seat leaving Martin to place an impotent knee on the seat and a finger on the wheel.

'I'm driving?'

'Yes. Get in. It's cold.'

'I'd rather you drove.'

'Why, can't you?'

The dent gleamed in his tense forehead.

'Yes, but I'd rather you did if you don't mind.'

Clare thumped ungraciously into the driver's seat and some seconds after the other door had slammed turned to see Martin settling upright beside her with an expectant smile on his face.

'Where are we going?' she asked.

'Going?' His eyes slewed round to confront her.

'Oh, I see. We're just going to sit here all night, are we?'

'No, of course not,' he improvised wildly. 'There's a

very nice little pub at Henton where they have draught cider and the food's very good. I thought we might drive out there. All right?'

Clare's sigh was lost in the start of the engine. She realized that some sort of idiot was occupying the seat beside her with fists clenched on knees, staring desperately into the lights of Henton below them. Then a drab oasis, a withered bay tree in a pool of light —

'I say, look, there it is, the Rising Sun. Stop!'

'Weren't you expecting it, then?'

A plastic clothes line was stretched across the entrance to the grit car park. Clare parked outside. She strode into the door and let it swing back, cutting off Martin, and stood alone on a prickly mat facing a pockmarked dartboard.

'Yes?' said a voice from the bar, and Martin came in to find Clare fixed in the stare of a great Alsatian with horny claws splayed on the bar and its tongue dripping on to a beer mat.

'Yes?'

A woman, her muzzle level with the dog's and as hostile, faced Martin who fumbled with the names of drinks until 'draught cider' rolled thickly off his tongue. The woman turned to get two glasses and displayed a tongue of black hair in a net on her neck between silver lurex shoulder blades. Clare retreated to a bench beneath a row of imitation horse brasses tacked through a belt on to the wall. The woman put the glasses on the counter and replaced the dog's beer mat with a dry one. As they slopped yellow cider rhythmically into their mouths to prevent speaking, Clare became aware, in the lull between elbow and mouth, of the loud ticking of a clock and looking round saw the peak of a cap protruding from the other side of a grandfather clock. The peak tipped backwards and a glass of mild held in an earthy hand appeared, tilted and disappeared. Clare nudged Martin who, unused to physical contact, swallowed a gulp of cider which flooded his throat, nose and eyes and she looked away. Two boots now jutted beyond the clock; Martin drowned its tick with spluttering.

'Finished?'

'Yes, thanks.'

'Good, because I've finished my drink.'

Martin leapt to the bar, clashing the glasses together.

'I say,' he said when he got back, 'there's a man sitting over there.'

'Congratulations.'

'What did your parents think when you told them you were going out with me?'

'How should I know what they think?'

'I just wondered because, I mean, my mother would go absolutely bonkers.'

'Oh, really. I didn't know the thought of me was enough to drive people's mothers bonkers.'

'Oh, she doesn't like me either,' he reassured her. 'Because of your father, I mean.'

'How old are you anyway?'

'Wrong side of thirty. Twenty-seven actually.'

'When's your birthday?'

'September the twenty-fifth.'

'Oh, you're a Libra.'

'Better not let Mother hear you say that.'

'Surely she must know?'

'Oh, she doesn't. She's a true-blue dyed-in-the-wool

Conservative, you see. If she found out she'd have me taken off the electoral roll and I've only just got on it.' He rose unsteadily.

'Call the hag over,' said Clare loudly.

'Same again please!'

After a long moment, during which Clare searched in her handbag and Martin drew in spilled cider on the table, she bent down and sixty inches of silver hip-straining behind emerged panting on their side of the bar. While she stood with her hand extended for the money, Clare stuck her long legs out like an affront and Martin's fingers floundered in the fluff in his pockets. The wind rushed against the pub walls, the moaning in the telegraph wires rose to a wail and, as if in answer, the telephone shrieked behind the bar. Martin pulled out some change, the woman grabbed it without looking and thrust it into a pouch in her skirt, and revealing mottled ankles was back behind the bar hissing into the receiver. She cradled it on a lump of lurex and said to Martin and Clare:

'We're closed. You'll have to go.'

Martin rose but Clare looked at the clock – it said twenty to nine. She drained her glass and sighed and stood up too. The cap behind the clock didn't move.

'Well what are you waiting for? We're not wanted here.' Clare strode to the door and flung it open to a blast of rain. She was at the wheel of the car listening to Martin blundering through a puddle when she realized he had been let off too lightly for the dismal evening.

'Oh Martin, I seem to have left my purse in the pub.'

'Oh God, how much was in it?'

'About three pounds.'

'Are you sure you haven't got it?'

'Positive.'

'I didn't notice it in the pub.'

'It's all I've got till the end of the week. What shall I do?'

'Just tap on the window and ask her if she's found it. Slip her sixpence.'

'I daren't. You go, Martin.'

'Look, supposing I was to lend you the money.'

'My library tickets are in it.'

'Which library?'

'Oh go on, Martin. What's the matter with you?'

Light blazed from the window and was extinguished by a shutter. His heart and feet were heavy as he crunched across to the pub. At the door he turned back desperately to Clare's profile and heard the click of her cigarette lighter above the rain sluicing round him.

Tap, tap. Laughter within gurgled to a spitting sound and stopped. The bolt was drawn back and glowering weakly beneath his cap stood the ugliest man Martin had ever seen. He wore a long khaki greatcoat and looked like a soldier from an obsolete army. Glasses in amber plastic frames were hooked round huge fleshy ears sprouting ginger forests and on a gross snout above swinging purple lips.

'I say,' began Martin.

'No you don't,' replied the other crashing a fist into his face and swinging back his arm for another blow which missed because Martin had fallen at the first.

'Get up.' He pulled him by the tie to his feet and, into Martin's gasping, purple pleading face, 'You're Oates, aren't you?'

'No.'

Finger and thumb clamped on Martin's nose and he danced on the wet grit flailing his arms and knocking over the bay tree and tub which fell on his attacker's foot and was kicked away.

'You're Oates, aren't you?'

'Yes.'

He released his nose and Martin cradled it in his hand with tears pouring over his fingers.

'You and your mother have got a lot to answer for, haven't you?' His pincers flashed out.

'Yes.'

'Tell your mother to keep away from Coral Fairbrother.' He twisted Martin round by the nose and sent him sprawling with a kick. Martin crawled back to the car.

'Get up, you oaf. Did you get it?'

'No.'

'That's hardly surprising. I found it in my pocket after you'd gone. By the way, your nose is bleeding.'

At a bend in the hill Martin's head suddenly crashed on to her shoulder, knocking her hands from the wheel, and the car hit the side of the road, mounted the bank, shot across the top of a silo, overturned in the field below and lay on its roof with spinning wheels.

*   *   *

'It's a nice friendly little ward, only four beds,' said the young nurse, when Clare woke, wearing a hospital nightdress in a high iron bed with scarlet blankets.

'There's nothing wrong with me.'

'I'll be the judge of that,' rasped an Irish brogue from the head of the bed.

'I've explained that she's got slight concussion and bruises,' apologized the nurse.

'Concussion my foot!'

Clare turned to look at Sister and saw a straight blue back stalking away on little legs.

'How long will I have to stay here? What sort of ward is it?' she asked in panic, but the nurse had gone. Two girls lay opposite with bottles of blood suspended above their beds; a woman beside her seemed to be asleep. A sparrow with a feather in its beak flew past the window, the scent of a pink hyacinth on the sill was blown across her bed. She took it for granted that Martin must be dead, for landing her in this humiliating position. A sobbing sound came from a bed opposite and weary words of comfort were followed by the thud of a box of tissues on the floor.

'Don't worry about me, I'll be all right,' blubbered a voice amid more sobs, and the crying continued. 'I've never been away from my John before.'

'I've never been away from Bob.'

'Yes, but it's different for me. I'm too sensitive. Will they cut me open, Doctor?' she wailed as a doctor made his round. Clare wondered why he ignored the woman next to her and turned on her side to sneak a glance. She could have stared all day and it wouldn't have mattered. The sheet had slipped back and a plastic face lolled sightlessly towards her; a tank with dials was attached by tubes to the bed. Lunch was served. Clare's soup grew cold, untouched, while she thought of the grave into which Martin must soon be lowered. Stella Oates, on a coconut mat brought out from the vestry, stood nearest the brink, a black lace handkerchief in a black glove; and at the edge of the little crowd, in a long black coat borrowed from her mother, stood Clare, screwed into the grass by her heels. She unscrewed herself and walked down the path through the lych gate and past the assembled village who stood back silently, a shower of confetti fluttered on to her gleaming hair – she had got confused with the scene of the assembled village greeting the popular and radiant bride – 'I didn't know I had so many friends,' she murmured.

She looked up into Sister's clean-shaven jaw.

'Nurse, my friend who was in the accident with me – could you find out when the funeral is?'

'What are you talking about, funeral? He's in the General Booth ward drinking his soup large as life which is more than can be said for some people.'

Clare obediently clattered her spoon in the cold scum tasting of carrots. Metal-covered dishes were approaching on a trolley and Sister had apparently decided to stay.

'What do you think this is?' she asked, waggling her frilled cap.

'A hat?'

'It means that I have attained the rank of Sister, and I'll thank you to remember it. What's this, roast beef?'

She lifted the cover and sniffed at a pool of gravy.

'Come on, eat up, it's all fresh meat from the operating theatre. Never mind me, I must have my little joke. Isn't that right, Staff?' she shouted across the ward.

'Yes, Sister?'

'I must have my little joke.'

'Yes, Sister.'

After lunch, which she was not allowed, one of the girls was collected by two men and taken away on a trolley. When she was returned to her bed she was alseep. Her anaesthesia was broken by a voice.

'Don't worry about me, I'll be all right.'

'What's the matter with her?' said Clare to the nurse, indicating the woman beside her.

'She's been like that for two years. She occasionally wakes up and cries a little, that's all.'

As the hours dragged on it seemed inconceivable to Clare that her life should not drain away like tomato soup or blood.

*   *   *

'Mummy, Daddy, take me away from here,' she sobbed, pouring herself like putty into her parents' delighted hands.

'That's what we've come for, darling.'

Joan and Dennis drove home in a pleasant glow in the righted Mini with Clare trembling on the seat beside her mother, who from time to time inclined towards her with a query which was not answered.

Chapter Twenty-two

The last of the chicken wire was ripped from the window frame leaving twenty skinned fingers writhing; a Council official plunged through the opening in an ineffectual cloud of self-raising flour and the siege was over. Inside the room all the furniture was piled against the door, a pool of glass splinters testified to the struggle. The Cheeseman family was being evicted from the last of a row of three cottages; the land was scheduled for redevelopment by Stella Oates.

At the edge of the crowd in the front garden stood Stella with a petal from the almond tree lying lightly on her hair. The Cheesemans filed out, acknowledged the cheers with weary jerks of the head, flashed smiles of bravado at the reporters and began to supervise the loading of their furniture on to the lorry that was to take it to Mrs Cheeseman's sister's, which was to be their unhappy home. One of them was missing; Grandfather, who had organized the siege, refused to leave the house where he had been born and they thought it best not to mention him. As she turned away lest she be spat at, Stella heard lambs in the field above and remembered that she must tell the farmer to move them in case they kept her awake.

A path where pools of sky floated among the flints, a tract of treacherous green where each step might plunge into frogspawn and a patch of reed mace that rasped when the wind rose separated these cottages from the one where Coral watched the eviction from an upstairs window which she slammed down so hard that the frayed rope sash broke. The house was falling apart, Stella closing in on her. The heartless voices of the children came up from the celandines below; she could bear the house no longer and started walking towards Henton woods.

She sat at the base of an elm with old dark pools in its roots where blind lice swam or drowned in the stinking leaves. Diffuse light steamed from the wood below. She picked a way down and found thousands of primroses with pink stalks like young rabbits' ears in the pale sun among the moss and flints and pits wrenched from the earth by falling trees. The blue macadam road to Henton ran alongside the wood and Coral jumped down with ringing ankles. Behind her on the road she saw Paula and Ralph behind the pram and sat down to wait for them to cover the half mile.

* * *

Sometimes, especially on Sunday mornings like this, Clare wished she was more friendly with the village girls. Today, as usual, they stopped talking at her approach, and bursts of laughter assailed her back. She noticed as she strode past in walking shoes how the gap between their and her age had widened. Where had her contemporaries gone? Had she known them better she would also have known that almost nothing would have induced them to walk in the woods near Henton, whose chalky approach she had left and over whose sulphurous wild arum leaves burning through ground ivy she now walked blindly, unaware that it was here that a Brownie pack was brutally attacked.

Her thoughts were wrenched downwards by a tasselled shoelace tangling in wet grass and bending to release it she saw she had come out of the wood. She saw in front of her a white narcissus edged with red. She had seen strayed daffodils and sweet peas on charred chalk railway banks but never narcissus in an open field. Not a yellow water-iris but an exotic purple brushed her skirt. She crossed a barbed-wire fence hung with rose leaves and vetch, jumped on to lusher grass, and almost fell over a mossy stone ball and was tottering on the top step of a broken flight of steps before she realized she was falling into a sunken garden. A heap of blackened bricks on her right, a dank maze buzzing with midges on her left, were the remains of Henton House bombed twenty years ago. The sun-dried almond blossom was like newly hatched wings, an early bee walked round the dry bed of a fountain, but her eyes were drawn to the maze. She walked slowly down one side, running her hand along the soot-generating yew leaves until she came to an entrance, and threw a tear-stained handkerchief on to the hedge and started walking, from time to time looking over her shoulder at the handkerchief lying like a grey beacon to direct her back.

She stopped, head halfway through a natural gap, blackened hands holding back the red branches, and listened. A slight wind along the sombre corridor lifted the hair from her ears and she heard a voice so close that her heart leaped as she turned to see who was talking to her. But the maze was silent and the voice went on and was joined by another. Children. She forced herself to walk on. Light broke through the hedge and leaves of light lay on the path; she was approaching an outer wall and the voices were louder through a single barrier of yew. Through the branches she saw lying with her cubs in the grass her mother's former cleaning woman, unaware that a monster was emerging from the bed of the old canal and trailing green slime across the grass. Clare crouched, poised to save herself, her speech to the coroner racing through her head. He passed within inches of her but she did not recognize Martin's attacker from the pub. He called out a greeting, swung a sack from his shoulder to the ground, and removed his cap as Coral rolled over.

'Ah, Elf,' Clare heard, and moved closer. 'I thought you were never coming.'

'I had to help out in the bar.' Elf stooped to untie his sack, something glittered in his hand, Clare swallowed a scream as he plunged a sandwich in cellophane towards Coral's heart. The children sat at a distance while Elf tossed them bags of crisps which crackled in the grass.

'Bring out the pickled eggs, Elf.'

Elf's head glistened as he unwrapped the bluish eggs from a paper napkin.

'I've been thinking, Elf, now that we are engaged, would you prefer me to call you George?'

'No.' He placed a whole egg in his mouth and churned it on his lips.

'Why not?'

'My name's John. Any news from your solicitor yet?'

'He says he's beginning to see daylight.'

'Did he really, beginning to see daylight, eh? Not long now then, eh?'

'Don't be so intense, Elf. Haven't you brought anything to drink?'

He pulled out a bottle of beer. Clare watched with distaste as the dark bottle was tilted first to mother's then to children's lips, the dregs sufficed Elf who raised the bottle with an audible glug and discarded it over his shoulder. It struck Clare on the brogue. She raised her knees from the cold mud and as she turned away Elf, an absent-minded finger twirling the whiskers in his ear, was leaning earnestly towards Coral who was salting a bag of crisps.

*　　*　　*

'Clare! Thank God. We're just in time for church if we leave now.'

Joan had suggested that it would be a nice gesture if the family went to church to show their gratitude for Clare's preservation.

Behind the sparse row of boys in the choir stalls two old sisters faltered the hymn desperately with a look of the slaughterhouse in their eyes, as if they knew they were to be called into the vestry after the service. Suddenly Miss McNaught stopped singing and her sister quavered to a halt and followed her stare. The congregation in the cold stone nave heard the door click behind them but went on singing. There was some sniggering in the choir stalls and a hymn book fell as a boy leaned forward to look. Clare turned her head. An

apparition came clanking up the aisle. It was Martin
Oates with his leg in plaster. To her horror he hoisted
himself into their pew, sidled up to her and placed a
hand on her hymn book and raised his voice in praise.
Clare let go. Disembodied pages spilled from the hymn
book's spine and she stood rigid as the verses ground
on.

During the sermon she glanced at Martin and saw
that he was leaning back, eyes closed, cast resting stiffly
on a hassock and a superior smile on the half of his
mouth not obscured by Elastoplast. Clare opened her
handbag and wrote on the flyleaf of her ivory covered
prayer-book with the pencil from her diary: 'Get out of
our pew,' and passed it to him. He waved it away,
scarcely lifting his hand from the worn red cushion.

The blessing had been asked and people were rising
from their knees to music from the organ. Clare did not
need the scrape of the cast to know that Martin was behind her.

'Glad to see you out and about again,' said Dennis,
who had occasionally seen Martin slinking about the
village.

Martin didn't notice that he had elbowed Joan into
the nettles as they walked along the road. When they
reached their gate she looked down and saw white
bumps swelling under her stocking.

'Well, goodbye, Martin. We mustn't keep your
mother waiting.'

'Indeed not,' said Dennis heartily.

'Oh that's all right. I'm not in any hurry.' He held the
gate open and the family had to troop through.

Joan and Clare toyed with their forks, Dennis raised his, saw that Martin was mumbling over his plate and went on eating.

'Actually, Clare, I'm jolly grateful to you,' Martin said, attacking his food.

'Oh really. Well, I can't say Clare's mother and I are very grateful to you and what's more I think you owe Clare an apology, to say the least. You have inquired neither about Clare's health nor the car which you nearly succeeded in wrecking, nor attempted to explain how the accident occurred.'

'Just a moment,' said Martin, smiling. 'Wait till you hear what I've got to say. Pass the wine please, Clare. I'm going to ask Clare to be my wife.'

'Out of my house!' roared Dennis, decanting the bottle over Martin's head.

He fled dripping and suffused with wine and disbelief to dry off in the recreation ground and was attacked by a mob of children. He raised his hands to bless them and a dead bird smote him in the face. Martin passed the rest of the afternoon in meditation in his wine-soaked clothes in his bedroom.

* * *

'What's all this nonsense about not going back to work, Martin?'

'I have been given other work to do.'

'Don't be so ridiculous. I've been in touch with your firm and they expect you back tomorrow. They don't seem to regard you as indispensable. I got the impression they didn't know who you were.'

Martin opened his prayer-book and Stella withdrew her head.

'By the way,' she said, 'you won't come down next week-end, will you? I've got some of the W.V.S. staying for Easter.'

'I shall be living here from now on.'

'Well you won't be next week-end. Your room has been requisitioned.'

Martin remembered a freezing childhood night when he had crept down from the attic where he had been billeted and had opened his bedroom door and seen by torchlight a pair of scaly grey feet lying stiffly on his sheet.

'You're too late, Mother, that room's already been requisitioned. By me.'

'You wouldn't be so silly as to try to fight me. The past must have taught you that.'

'Times have changed, Mother,' said Martin gently. 'You must try to move with them.'

'Get out of my house.' She snatched the prayer-book and threw it at Martin's exposed toes. It bounced off the cast.

'You jolly well wait,' he heard his voice blubber up through the years.

*   *   *

The grass was white, the flowering currant bombarded with white shot, the path bouncing as Dennis ran home in a hailstorm on Monday evening and stood panting in the hall.

'That oaf Oates nearly got me – managed to shake

him off in the King's Arms. There's a pint waiting for me on the bar which I shall never drink.'

Joan touched her leg in irritation and white stings blazed in a field of red.

Chapter Twenty-three

'Christ is risen!' said Stella looking up from her paper.
  'What?'

The first arrival for breakfast froze in the doorway, incredulous joy blazing from her face.

'An old Easter greeting,' Stella explained.

'Of course. How silly of me.' She spread out her green skirt and sat down.

'I think we'll give the others another few minutes, don't you?' said Stella, who had set her alarm for seven in order to discomfit her guests.

The sun struck the mirror that was an ornamental pond in Stella's Easter garden on the sideboard, momentarily blinding her guest, who shielded her glasses and went over to investigate. A family of lead ducks swam across the pool towards a mossy tomb with gaping mouth and a flint close by, and through the primroses, not a day older and wearing the same chipped blue-and-white dress she had worn at the Nativity, came the Virgin Mary.

The rest of the group, disturbed by the constant activity in the bathroom, trooped through the door and sat round the table. One chair was empty. There was a general laugh. A lady with wild grey hair dashed in with a pyjama leg dripping out below her skirt.

'Oh Stella!' Then they all gasped. A real pheasant sat on a nest in the centre of the table. Stella lifted it to expose a clutch of painted eggs.

'Oh, it's stuffed. No wonder its eyes are closed.'

Stella removed the eggs and replaced the bird; each one had a name painted on its shell. She dealt them out amid cries of appreciation. The bright feathers glittered, the beak slumped contentedly on the breast. The last lady down to breakfast paused in cracking the egg named Miss Trigg. There was something disconcerting about the long yellow tail feathers and the red patch round the sunken eye.

'Surely it's a cock bird?' she whispered.

'Pheasant!' hissed her neighbour.

*   *   *

A naked egg lay on every plate among coloured fragments of shell. Meanwhile the grapefruits languished. When Stella noticed their mistake, the ladies dipped silver spoons into their grapefruit, except Miss Trigg who had eaten her grapefruit and her egg and had to sit with working jaws making a mosaic of eggshell on her plate and from time to time sipping the tea-leaves from her drained cup.

Stella, slimmest of all in her waisted green jacket, handed round buttered toast laboriously made on the ancient stove in the kitchen at cost to the hired woman of a burned hand and several ounces of sweat.

'I thought I got unsalted butter,' murmured Stella to herself.

The ladies felt more at ease now and the faint aura

they had taken for Stella's saintliness they now perceived to be damp.

A scarecrow fresh from the field burst in with a wet patch on one knee and wisps of grass trailing from the bare toes of the other foot. Stella saw her breakfast party crumble like eggshells around her.

'Happy Easter, everybody. Don't worry, Mother, I've just come to collect something.'

He swung across to a cupboard and took out a banner and went out again with the words, 'Good hunting.'

A grand egg-hunt in the garden was planned for after church.

Chapter Twenty-four

'It's the olden days and you're my brother and I'm your sister, you've just come home from hunting and I have to ask you what you've shot and you have to say, "Nothing."'

Ralph plodded a few feet up the path and returned to the chalk cave in the roots of a fallen elm.

'What, up already, Brother?'

'It's way past cock-crow, Sister,' he repeated dully.

'Did you shoot anything?'

'No.'

'Do you think any travellers will pass our way that we can rob, Brother?'

No travellers ever passed their way and the game seldom progressed further.

'I will climb to our look-out post,' said Ralph, pulling himself up on to the trunk.

'Paula!'

A jaunty little head in a scarlet cap was bobbing along between the nettles. Paula crept along the trunk and swung from a branch, knocking him to the path; a treble whistle pierced the pursed red lips as his head thudded to the mud.

'Bring the prisoner into the cave.'

Ralph climbed down stolidly and placing a not unkind hand on the scarlet collar pulled him to his feet and pushed him into the cave. His fall had knocked a tear from each eye.

'Name?'

'Simon Slim.'

'Age?'

'Seven years and three months.'

*   *   *

Light drained from the sky into black hedges and fences, the river ran coldly over the stones. Ralph looked at the tear-stains running from the closed lids of the prisoner lying on a pile of leaves.

'Shall we go home now?'

A bony implacable leg swung from the tree above.

'You can, I'm not.'

'Why not?'

'Somebody's got to guard the prisoner.'

'Let him go then.'

'How can we? He'll report us.'

'We could just leave him here.'

She jumped down but they had not gone far when they were stopped by a wail, 'Wait for me.'

'Run for it!'

A well-fed hand shot out and brought Ralph down. Simon Slim looked at his captors' turnip-lantern faces in the dusk.

'Let me come with you.'

'Go home to your mummy, little boy,' said Paula coldly.

'I'll just come a little way with you and then I'll go

home,' he said confidently and accompanied them in silence to their house.

'You've got to go home now.' Paula stood with her arms stretched across the gate.

'Paula! Ralph! Where the hell have you been?'

They recognized that voice from a terrible evening when they had been playing in the maze and Elf suddenly lurched out at them from a yew tree saying he was their new daddy and their mother appeared staggering and screeching in the snow at the mouth of the maze and flung a bottle at Elf's head.

'Get away!' she hissed at the prisoner and dragged Ralph through the gate. Simon climbed over.

'I want to come to tea with you.' He could not remember why he had not gone to school; he feared the darkness less than home.

Paula grabbed the prisoner by the hand and dragged him down the garden to the hen-house, pushed him in, dropped the wooden latch and went simpering with fear into the kitchen where her mother turned ginny eyes, rolling between smiles and tears, towards her. Paula sidled past her upstairs to the rags she called her bed.

'Where's the prisoner?'

'Cast into the deepest dungeon.'

Elf's voice came from the back door.

'Tonight, Coral?'

'Don't be absurd, Elf.'

*   *   *

When he found himself face downwards on the lumpy floor of the shed Simon did not cry, although it was almost pitch dark, for two reasons. At the age of four he had been sent off to school by bus in an enormous cap, not knowing the name of his destination. In the three subsequent years his head had grown but the size of his successive red caps had not, and he had become a stoic on his evening descent from the bus and the walk home, with his giant cow-hide satchel bumping resolutely on his back, past his contemporaries who had been home from school an hour. The second reason was that he would soon be discovered, rescued and probably pronounced too tired for school the following day. He decided to say that he had gone to look for daffodils for his mother's birthday, got lost and taken shelter in the chicken-house. Of Ralph and Paula he would say nothing because he feared their goblin faces and their revenge. He ran his hand over the floor and felt feathers and straws, he knelt up and placed his face to the little wire netting window and watched for some movement at the back door of the house drowning in grass. He heard something move behind him and as he turned saw a chink of light close and stretched out his hand. Valerie the hen saw a finger wriggling towards her like a worm, lunged a hungry beak and seized it.

* * *

Stella, lying in the dark house with its profusion of moths whose papery wings rustled like the honesty seeds outside, was woken by her front door bell at two o'clock. She could hear rain on the roof and presumed that Martin had lost his key and was begging for shelter.

'You can sleep in the shed,' she shouted. The bell

rang again and she was forced to descend the wide staircase and saw Martin's frightened face appear at his door. She pulled back the stained-glass door as far as the chain allowed and saw two men under the porch light.

'Sorry to get you up, Mrs Oates, but a little boy's missing. We want to search your garden.'

'How terrible. Of course.'

'Any sheds or wells, Mrs Oates?'

'One shed — it's halfway down the garden. Is it one of the village children?'

'No, it's Mr Slim's son.'

'I'll come down and help you look,' called Stella after them into the dark garden before closing the door and returning to bed.

The two men, after searching the shed, spent fifteen uneasy minutes waiting for Stella, during which time Simon could have fallen into the river ninety times.

She did not hear the whistle shrieking through the dawn to recall the search parties. A little scarlet-and-gold figure propelled by unseen hands had stumbled through the mist into the bowed heads of four men beating the grass with long sticks. Neither his mother tucking him into bed nor his father, excusing himself from the celebration and coming upstairs with moist ginger eyes and a cut-glass tumbler of whisky, could persuade him to tell where he had been.

Chapter Twenty-five

Flu had raged through the two classrooms and closed the school. The day it reopened Mr Evans, the Attendance Officer, ashen from a prolonged attack of jaundice, parked his car outside the school, crossed the playground, slipped on a sliver of soap outside the cloakroom and hit his head on the drain. He turned round and staggered back to his car where he was found slumped at playtime and driven to the hospital and admitted with a fractured skull.

A week later Miss Jigger, wearing a light-weight spring suit slightly tight at the waist, with a bunch of violets rammed under the pin of her brooch by a misguided pupil, appeared with her register in Mr Gutteridge's classroom as he was leaving.

'Could I have a word with you, Mr Gutteridge?'

He followed her into her classroom and confronted the wilting violets on her lapel.

'Don't you think ... ?' he said.

'All right Peter, you may go,' said Miss Jigger to the boy who stood on the nature table with a waste-paper basket on his head. He got down stiffly.

'What are we going to do about the Fairbrothers? Paula's been absent for months and there's a younger brother who should probably have started school by now, and the beginning of term is the best time to act.'

'Better wait till Evans gets back. It's his province.'

'Goodness knows when he'll be back. He'll probably break his neck on the way back from the operating theatre.'

'Oh, I hope not. I take it you want me to summons the mother? Well, these things have to go through the proper channels, you know.'

'If you won't do anything I will. Those children run around like savages with leaves and berries in their hair.'

Her brown shoes keeled over on the flints as she walked down the lane. A bat flew over the fence, Miss Jigger screamed and ducked her head against the rusty railing, a cold tendril of bryony plucked her mouth, cold nettles discharged sacs of poison into her stockings, she beat at her pleat of hair long after the bat had circled away. When she had straightened and rammed a slipped hair clip into her head she set off again with ill-humour over-riding her sense of purpose and she jarred her arm pushing the gate against the grass.

For ten minutes she stood, legs on fire, pleat of hair sliding, knuckles ringing, knocking in vain. She saw that the handle hung loosely and a screw lolled out of its socket. She turned the handle and paused on the wormy threshold smelling the damp and thought for a moment the house had been abandoned. Withered bulrushes and teasel stood in a vase on a three-legged table, drab rags hung at the windows, legless chairs leaned against the walls.

'It would be interesting to see what the larder contains,' she thought, going into the other room. She opened a cupboard door and screamed. Stella Oates, blue-haired and blue-suited, stepped out and smiled.

'I came in the back door,' she explained. 'I'm trespassing too.'

Hands fluttering, tongue bulging with relief, Miss Jigger leant against the wall. 'Isn't it foul,' she stuttered, her nails picking blisters of damp and rolling crumbs of plaster on the wall behind her.

'It's Miss Jigger, isn't it? I'm Stella Oates. I was one of the school managers once, before your time.'

Beside this neat dragonfly Miss Jigger felt her asymmetrical body sag and a stocking crease in the ridges round her ankle, felt her hair slipping down, put out a hand to save it and it cascaded weakly down, scarcely scraping her shoulders.

'I'm sorry, what did you say?' she asked, as Stella looked at her expectantly.

'I asked what induced you to break into this hovel.'

'The door was open – I did knock, you must have heard me. Actually I came here officially, to warn Miss Fairbrother that we intend to take legal action if she doesn't send her children to school.'

'Quite right. Shall we peep upstairs?'

'Oh, we couldn't.'

'Careful, some of these stairs are rotten.'

They were so steep that Miss Jigger had to revert to all fours and was piqued to see Stella arrive upright on the tiny landing between the rooms.

'This must be the children's room.' Stella looked round from the doorway and stepped into the other room.

'Sheets, such as they are, reasonably clean,' said Miss

Jigger and looked round for a mirror to adjust her skirt but found none.

'So this is the famous boudoir.'

'Haystacks and ditches more likely. What on earth have they done with all the furniture?'

'Burned it.'

'Honestly, some people aren't fit to be called civilized; the modern equivalent of keeping coal in the bath.'

Miss Jigger was scrabbling through a pile of clothes in a corner – she held up a coat and hooted.

'Latest Paris fashion,' she said, poking her arm into the sleeve and twirling round. Stella picked up a black scarf and held it round her face.

'Saintly Sister Maria!' shrieked Miss Jigger. A polka-dot dress sent her into convulsions.

'What is it?' Stella asked, growing alarmed.

'There must be five yards of material in this skirt,' she managed to choke at last. 'To complete the ensemble, a pair of size eight gumboots.' She thrust her foot into one of a pair of encrusted boots. Her heel jammed in the stem.

'Something's stuck in the toe.'

'A mouse?'

Miss Jigger screamed and lay on the bed kicking her feet together and feeling fur and bones rattle against her toes.

'What was that noise?'

Miss Jigger didn't hear, she was sitting on the floor grunting and pulling the boot with both hands, all the time expecting teeth to nip through the nylon. Stella dragged her to the landing, she slipped and the wooden stairs bumped down her spine and she arrived with a boot at right angles to her leg at the feet of her former pupil, Paula.

'Mummy's dress!' She was on her like a ferret, ripping at the skirt, trying to drag it over Miss Jigger's head. A blow from Stella's elbow in her frail chest crashed her against the wall. Miss Jigger picked herself up and rushed out on crooked feet, the torn bodice of the dress exposing a smear of violet on the beige lapel.

Stella's car overtook her and she hobbled in the open door and sank back on the seat. She swelled again beside Stella's neat knees, her face still blotched with laughter, her boot shedding a crust of mud on the carpet under the dashboard. As they drove through Stella's gate she recovered sufficiently to say, 'Mummy's dress!' in a dying snort of laughter.

Stella pulled off the boot with her own hands and Miss Jigger's turnip-root feet crawled uneasily on the carpet. To her intense humiliation a crimson nail she had painted in a moment of boredom protruded from a hole and her face flushed to match. Stella left the room and she took advantage of her absence to leap up and examine her face in the glass of a picture but it was clouded with dust and she had just bounced back in her chair when Stella returned with a teapot.

'What are the penalties for keeping children from school? I'm afraid I'm rather ignorant of such matters. Is there a chance of the mother being jailed?'

'I'd have to ask Mr Gutteridge, he's the legal expert, but I think perhaps, yes. I seem to remember reading of a similar case where a mother of ten was jailed.'

'Ten? It seems very young.'

'No, I mean ten children.'

'This one's only got three, hasn't she?'

'Paula, a boy who should have started school, and that disreputable-looking baby. I've seen it in the garden, and if ever I saw evil in a child's face —'

When Miss Jigger left, promising to call again as soon as she had any news, she did not like to mention that she had no shoes and she set off down the gravel drive smiling and waving.

Chapter Twenty-six

Simon Slim had broken under questioning. A week had passed, most of which he spent in bed, the flea-bites above the permanent garter marks on his white legs indistinguishable from the chicken-pox that splashed his body.

The doctor had just left and Simon was turning over the page of a comic, with a bandaged finger, when his mother came into the room and sat with folded hands on his bed.

'Simon, I've been having a long talk with your formmaster.'

The bright squares of comic rushed together in panic. Simon looked up at his mother with unflinching blue eyes.

'It seems that you're not altogether an honest little boy. You told me that you had swopped that stamp for a British Guiana, but you took it. That was a sneaky thing to do, wasn't it, Simon?' The red spots fused on his molten face. 'And Mr Carstairs also tells me that you're a little bit ready to run to the masters with tales. In my day we called a person like that a creep.

'Of course, it makes no difference to Daddy and me, darling,' she said, putting an arm round his shaking shoulders. 'You'll stay here with us, still share the playroom with Nicky and Markie.'

The doorbell rang and she ran downstairs, leaving him burning and exposed on the pillow. When she returned his face, thick with viscous tears, was hidden and his shoulder-blades heaved through his pyjamas.

'I've always found, Simon, that when one has let someone down, the best way to put it right is to do something for them. I expect you'd like to tell us what happened the other night.'

*   *   *

'Do you know my wife? Joan, this is Mr Fairbrother.'

'Of course, we've often passed in the street.'

'You sit down here, Mr Fairbrother. I expect you could do with a drink.'

Dennis followed Joan into the kitchen.

'What on earth have you brought him here for?'

'Where's that bottle of beer we had?'

'He's not staying to dinner.'

'He had his dinner at twelve. Don't be so damned uncharitable.'

He found the beer at the back of a cupboard among the dusters.

'If you must know he was in danger of being lynched in the King's Arms. I had to get him away.'

'What did he do? Clare might be home at any minute.'

'Don't worry, it was nothing to do with him. It seems that Simon Slim was at Coral's that night, locked in a chicken-run.'

'Oh no.'

'Stella's been stirring it up in the village. The atmo-

134

sphere in the pub was explosive, the old boy was trembling like a leaf. They were throwing darts at his feet.'

Fairbrother was still shaking when Dennis returned with the beer; he clasped his knee to stop it and a cloud of dust rose from the withered corduroy. He sat drinking dully from the glass held in both hands, staring at exotic green-and-gold, frosted and ruby bottles glittering across the room, and opened his mouth, a fang of froth hanging from his gum, but no words came. Joan burst in. 'Hide him, quick!'

They each took an arm and pulled him to his feet. The feet outside pounded past.

'Go and warn Coral, I'll look after him.'

Dennis ran out and Joan pushed Fairbrother to the stairs. He could not lift his feet. She propped him against the wall, climbed two stairs, took him under the shoulder and dragged him up, his loose feet bumping each stair, and threw him across the double bed.

She leant panting against the wall, pools of sweat lying among her hair, and watched Fairbrother on the dark-blue quilt, his rigid knees bent over the edge and a length of blotched shin exposed.

The front-door knocker crashed, a voice shrieked through the letter-box, 'Where is he?'

Fairbrother's lower jaw fell, the tendons had snapped.

Joan thought he was dead and fled to the front door. She opened it and Mrs Fairbrother fell on to her.

'Mr Fairbrother please.'

'Upstairs.'

Joan collapsed in a chair and heard thuds above and two pairs of feet, one firm, one stumbling, on the stairs.

Mr Fairbrother passed the open door with his wife's

practised fist in his back and Joan was left, as so often, sitting in the aftermath of a slammed door.

She switched on the television to wait for Dennis and during a commercial rose to her feet in the knowledge that she had heard just one pair of feet go down the path. She opened the front door, expecting a lifeless Fairbrother to slide to the ground, but the doorway was empty. She stepped on to the path, only the blurred green hawthorns against the dark-blue sky, an emerald-and-ruby plane above, then she saw him slumped rustily over the chair. She raised his head and smelled alcohol on his fallen jaw. Dennis had killed him with the beer.

She searched his scratchy chest for a heart and found none. She braced herself, placed her hands under his arms and fell backwards; he was as light as paper. She propped him up in the car and saw a red weal rubbed along the underside of his jaw and round his neck into the white stubble.

When she felt the car shoot forward instead of stopping outside the doctor's she did not know if that had been her intention. It stopped outside the almshouses from which he had been removed some time ago, and Joan pulled Mr Fairbrother out and, holding him upright as possible, got him through the gate and into a deck-chair under the apple tree in the tiny garden.

As she drove home she thought of him, at peace in his kingdom in the apple blossom, except that a petal might drift into his open mouth, and for the disquieting red marks which he could not have made shaving because etiolated wisps wavered on to his collarless shirt.

*   *   *

'Where the hell have you been?'

'I just drove along the road to meet you – must have missed each other.'

'Yes, well I don't want you going out alone at night just now. Tell Clare too.'

'Why, what happened?'

'Nothing tonight. The birds had flown, except one hen. Luckily for them. I was nearly lynched, as it happens.'

'Darling! Did they have a rope?'

'Several. They decided to string that hen up when they found Coral had gone.'

'Oh no! They didn't, did they? How could you stand there and let them hang a defenceless hen, you brute? Please don't ever attempt to speak to me again.'

'Go and look in the kitchen,' he said wearily and sank into a chair.

That the hen had been strung up and cut down too late was Joan's first incorrect thought when she saw the heap of feathers on a cushion in a cardboard box: they had even started to pluck it. An eye opened: Joan fell forward on her knees and stroked the tiny skull with her finger. Half an hour later she returned to the sitting-room.

'She's had a terrible shock, but if she can last the night, she'll pull through.'

'You would have made a good nurse, Joan.' He pulled her towards him. 'Why are your finger-nails all black?'

'I was looking for a worm.'

'Oh! I say, is there any of that cold chicken left, I'm starving.'

Joan went into the kitchen.

'Oh God!'

A grey corduroy cap lay on a chair. She picked it up; the ridges were stiff with dirt and the rusty stud had nearly corroded itself through the cloth.

She washed her hands and made Dennis's sandwich.

'I'm going to meet Clare,' she said and fled with the cap in a paper bag.

'Take the car,' she heard as she pounded through the gate.

She slowed down when she saw a group of women straggling across the road ahead of her; she was afraid of any two village women and often heard laughter as she greeted them and hurried past. She did not know any of them but knew that their hands were stained with hops and strawberries, they made pigeon pies and kept rabbits in the back garden to make into gloves. Try as she might she couldn't stop her feet from gaining on them and had to feign a stone in her shoe and bent down with the blood beating in her face in case they looked round. Mesmerized by grass, with dandelions exploding in her eyes, she straightened and resumed walking at her usual pace and was almost with the women at the allotment gate. They shouted something to someone over the fence and went on, laughing.

Leaning over the fence staring down the road into the misty rain was Mr Fairbrother.

'You're alive!' she cried, running forward and seizing his hand. It slipped from hers like a wet leaf. Along the allotments hung lines of drops that turned to a sheet of prisms as she flung the cap: it slid down the pearly wall of a greenhouse and lodged on an old encrustation of snails.

*   *   *

'Dennis, where does Mr Fairbrother live?'

'Beside the river with his wife – why? And where's Clare?'

Joan went heavily upstairs, where she spent a terrible night thinking of the old dead man who had been abandoned three times that day. Twice she got up to see if it was raining.

Old Mrs Fairbrother woke suddenly when her head fell forward on to her knees. She heard the river rushing past in the darkness and knew that she was still in her chair and Fairbrother had not returned from Blake's garden where she had left him in his senile stupor.

She groped with her feet for her misshapen shoes, lost one under the chair and closed her eyes again.

Dennis was woken by birdsong at 4 a.m. and could not get back to sleep; he took his clothes into the bathroom and dressed.

Fairbrother's hands had slipped from the gate and he lay where sorrel had sprung up round the rusty corrugated iron as Dennis passed the allotments' hedge and looked over a blaze of green and gold.

He opened the back door, the catch was broken, and went upstairs and stood on the little landing outside the room he had not entered since he bound up Coral's shot leg. She lay aslant on the bed, the spring sun curdling on her white neck where her hair had fallen over her face. He took off his shoes, crept into the heap of creaking rags and, his trousered knees against her sleeping side, fell fast asleep.

Chapter Twenty-seven

The Union Jack drooped over the village hall in a sky already burning blue when Dennis returned home – and passed his usual travelling companions on their way to the station.

'No, I won't be late because I'm not going,' he said to Joan.

'Oh well, I'm helping at the British Legion party this afternoon.'

'Is that why the flags are flying?'

* * *

There were many days when Joan would have welcomed having Dennis at home but today because she had made plans her resentment drove him out to the front garden to linger under the red hawthorn tree and grip a low branch with foreboding while a blackbird sang above and sweat gathered in his crushed shirt. Clare walked down the path in a white dress, glass cubes hanging at her ears, and stepped into her white car waiting like a refrigerator at the kerb.

When old Mrs Fairbrother arrived at the police station she was let into the kitchen by the policeman's wife and had to sit in a corner while the children suddenly put off their breakfast sat dumbly round the table, and giggled explosions of carbon dioxide bubbles into their milk. Down in the allotments their father was on his knees facing the doctor across Fairbrother's fallen jaw. A black slug with an orange frill rested on the cool earth by his hand under the hedge. The ambulance called by the commuter who had found him clashed through the village causing Mrs Fairbrother's cup to jump in its saucer and she had to rise and follow the departing bell down the street.

'These strange marks on his face,' she heard the doctor say, running his finger along the worn pink stripes. 'And his jaw seems to have broken. Of course in a case like this of advanced senility – Mrs Fairbrother! I'm afraid I've got some bad news for you.'

She looked at her husband lying in the grass; she knew her lines.

'Is he ... ?'

'I'm afraid so.'

Someone spread a coat for her on the grass. The doctor's finger on her husband's neck did not alarm her because she knew he had eczema behind his knees and the buckles on the muzzle on the kitchen wall would rust into the leather long after he was gone. Here in the quiet allotments among iron and tulips, seedlings and glass and compost, the ashes of a long-dead hay fever stirred, hot sparks clustered in her eyes and a molten tear dripped over the edge of each red crater.

*   *   *

'Elf! What are you doing here?'

What was he doing here? Elf stood braced in the

doorway in a short leather jacket and lumpy flannels, the bristles that flooded from his nose and ears crimson in the light streaming behind him.

'I don't know what you're talking about.'

'If you don't go I shall get out of bed.'

Elf retreated down four stairs.

'This time you don't get rid of me so easily.'

'Look, Elf, you must go. It isn't safe for you here today. Meet me at the old house at eight tonight.'

'You think I'm stupid, don't you? Well, I'm not going until you name the day.'

'Wednesday the twenty-fifth!'

Elf found himself plodding up the lane to Henton to consult the calendar in the bar and find that such a day would never dawn.

He stood at the door and rolled a cigarette and looked up from lighting it at the sound of a bell. Martin Oates was coming down the road at the head of a procession of children, holding a banner aloft and tinkling a little brass bell in the shape of a lady. He stuck the banner in the grass opposite the pub – Elf saw that it was a drawing of a sheep carrying a flag – and waited. A few adults joined the audience.

Martin read from a piece of paper, faltering over the first word.

'Friends. I bring you a message from the mouth of a dead man. As you may know, I was recently involved in a car accident, and I think I may say without boasting that I have been as close to death as anyone here. As I lay in my hospital bed, in the dead of night, just one dim light was flickering in the ward. An old, old geriatric suddenly took up his walking frame and wheeled it down the ward to my bed. His head – he had no hair – was shining like a halo. He put his head close to mine and whispered something in my ear. I grabbed his arm. He was quite dead. And this is the message the old man gave to me for you: "Go-o …" '

Elf had edged round and uprooted the banner and he broke it over Martin's head.

Chapter Twenty-eight

Though the village hall was a burning tin box and the apple blossom wilted in the vases round the wall, the pink, blue and lemon nylon dresses and the Brylcreem spikes of the under-fives seated at the trestle tables stood up stiffly. Joan was swilling pale orange squash into plastic cups, the older Miss McNaught circulated wilting jellies, and the younger, iced fancies. Stella stood at the top of the hall, rodent teethmarks in the cake on her plate. Three or four humble mothers stood round the walls.

Suddenly a child fell forward into his ice-cream and then another's head crashed down, making spoons jump along the table. The mothers rushed forward and the children were carried into the air outside. Another boy, his face as green as the watery jelly, rushed out. A mother with billowing skirt and the thin straps of her sandals breaking galloped down the road to the doctor's but was impeded when a heel sank into hot asphalt. Meanwhile two more children fainted and Stella, holding a boy's head between his knees, remarked to Miss McNaught that she had seen Coral Fairbrother sniffing round the refreshments earlier. Miss McNaught repeated it to her sister and was overheard, and soon hate for Coral which had been simmering since Simon Slim's confession, boiled more violently than the water in the hissing urn.

Mothers attracted by the cries of the woman trapped in the asphalt rushed in. The doctor arrived to find five children laid out like minnows on the grass, Stella's distracted blue head in the doorway of a room full of steam and a wraith wandering down the table spooning up the remaining jelly and ice-cream.

'It's just the heat,' he said as the last child sat up.

'If only we could believe that,' said Stella quietly. She insisted on driving each child home, although this meant a half-hour wait in the sun for some who lived five minutes' walk away, and poured her poison into the mothers' ears in the closed car.

'I expect your husband will want to take some action when he hears about this. Things have gone too far this time to be ignored.'

'As you say, Mrs Oates.' She and child were released from the swirling petrol fumes into the road.

'Mrs Oates! Mrs Oates!' Miss Jigger's face zoomed into the window and she opened the car door and thrust it in.

'I heard some of the children had been taken ill. I was stocktaking at school. Hang on, I'll just get in … I've had a super idea concerning you know whom.'

'I won't be needing you now, Miss Jigger.' She snapped the door shut, slicing the top of Miss Jigger's hair, and started the engine. Miss Jigger had to turn away down the lane in a blur of laurel leaves and walk back towards the school, each step knocking the tears nearer the rims of her eyes, under the truncated lacquer spurs.

'Miss Jigger.'

She recognized the voice of a pupil favoured for his hand-knit Fair Isle sweater and the Kirbigrip in his yellow hair.

'Shall I walk along the road with you?' His brown polished shoes strode along confidently an inch from the nettles. 'Miss Jigger, why don't you ever go home in the holidays?'

She tried to run, found his hand was in hers and left him lying bewildered face downward in the nettles.

●　　●　　●

'They've all gone, Moira.'

The old McNaught sisters stood alone in their uniforms in the village hall.

'We'll have to have the party on our own.' She put a paper hat on her sister's head.

'There's a batch of untouched jellies on the top table. Jings, Jeanie, the urn's burnt out.'

They each took a jelly and spoon and started to eat.

'Come on slowcoach, I've finished. I think a sandwich or two would go down well now.'

'You know I've got a very small mouth, I can't even get a banana in.'

She scraped a last splash of jelly from her chin and the tin spoon clattered on her teeth.

'Did you say those egg sandwiches went down well?'

'They're a wee bit tired. A glass of squash might help them down. Will I pour you one?'

'Oh Moira, my tummy wouldn't thank you for that. Just a wee tot then.'

'Well that was a nice wee tea!'

They wiped their little mouths on their handkerchiefs, a mound of topless sponges stood by the empty jug; the Misses McNaught had eaten off all the icing.

'Put your paper hat straight then, dearie.'

'Is that better?'

'A wee bit to the left I think. That'll do. I suppose we'd better go.'

'No games, Moira? That's not much of a party. You've forgotten how to enjoy yourself.'

'I have not. What shall we play?'

'Oh Moira, do you remember when we played "Water, Water Wallflower" at the Mackinnons' and Father said I was the belle of the ball?'

'He said I was the belle of the ball.'

But Jeanie's mind was dancing in a mist of Drambuie that golden Strathspey looking down into Father's laughing black eyes.

'Moira!'

She took her sister's hands and they began to sing.

> 'Water, Water Wallflower,
> Growing up so high
> We are all maidens
> And we must die,
> Except Jeanie McNaught —'

'Why did you say Jeanie?'

'Because you did.'

'You should have said Moira — what's that noise?'

Their paper hats fell off as they ran still hand in hand to the door. A mastiff-faced woman marched on either side of Mrs Slim who looked frightened, as if she had just been plucked from her kitchen. Behind them rolled half a dozen prams and fifteen more women, breaking step only to slap their children into line.

'What can they be doing?'

'Perhaps they're going maypole dancing on the village green.'

'There isn't one.'

'No.'

The air was filled with slaps and wailing as little legs were dragged along too fast and mothers anxious to show their determination pulled fallen babies to their feet. The Misses McNaught pinned their identical felt hats to their grey curls and hurried into the road where they were driven into the hedge and impaled on thorns by a car.

'Couldn't wait till our husbands got in, Mrs Oates,' a voice hit the window of the car.

Stella slowed down and took her place at the end of the procession. The members of a cycling club were trapped like butterflies behind.

The shrilling bells brought Joan and Dennis to the window.

'The mob! So it's risen again.'

'Don't be so theatrical, Joan.'

He rushed out, turned in the opposite direction from the procession, leaped over the allotment gate and ran across, tearing grass with his shoes and trampling tiny lettuces into the black earth. He crashed down on both feet on the gravel edge of the river and tried to run across but the current twisted his trousers round his legs, his feet slid on stones and he threw his hands forward to balance himself. His shin hit an iron bar, he fell and brown water and mud stirred by his own feet rushed into his eyes and ears and his chin hit a broken bottle. As he scrabbled on the slippery stones he was aware of an intolerable pain in his head and was drawn up by his hair, with streaming mouth and a deep red V running down his chin, to look out of flooded eyes at a long muddy leg braced to take his weight.

'You fool!' he said, pushing her back on the bank, and rose up from the slime. 'Come on, the vultures are at your house.'

He took her wrist and started to run again on sodden mud inner soles, pulling her with him. He did not hear her frail knees crack.

They reached the house, it was empty.

'Leave a note.'

'They can't read.'

She ran out into the lane and saw a great navy-blue pram turn down.

'Ralph! Paula! Stephen!'

The imprisoned cyclists burst free and sped round the corner. The leader struck a flint, bounced sideways, turned and locked antlers with the bicycle behind. The rest of the herd crashed about him in a heap of spokes and legs and gears and pennants. Some got up and replaced the coloured caps on their heads and disentangled the bicycles, some sat on the stones examining elbows and knees, one lay back while his bicycle was set on its wheels; a thick torrent of blood gushed from his knee. A handkerchief tourniquet was applied and he was swaying in his cycling shoes when the heavy blue pram drew up alongside and the mother pushing it was not quick enough and he sagged across the pram and was carried with it.

Coral was running wildly from room to room to the garden to the marshy field to the lane. Dennis caught her at the door.

'You get out of here, I'll wait for the children.'

'No. No. I must stay.'

She tried to push past him but was blocked by a barrage of chest.

'You don't know what those women are like! They'll tear you to pieces. Go!'

His slight push sent her spinning. She turned to scorch him with a look and turned into the lane.

'I'll take the children home with me,' he called.

From the doorway Dennis watched her march steadfastly towards the procession, her hair flame in the red sky. She stooped and picked up a flint, and flung it and walked on. It struck a dejected figure loitering in the hedge plucking at the wet leaves. Miss Jigger fell across the lane, anaemic blood from her thin epidermis splashing the dust.

A shout went up, the prams lunged forward, the women scooped up handfuls of stones. Coral saw the shower of black stones in the sky, turned and fled. Miss Jigger sat up, received the volley and sank back. Stella parked the car and sat back to watch.

* * *

Dennis shut the door and ran on shaking legs through the back door and over the fence into the field where he lay in a hollow with water soaking through the bright grass up his legs and jacket and closing in a cold ring round his neck.

'Break down the door!' It wasn't locked. A shoulder stuck in the splintered wood and had to be torn out.

'Allow me.'

The injured cyclist limped forward, turned the handle and fell back on the pram.

'Come on girls!'

'They're not here,' said Mrs Slim hopefully, and added, 'the rats.'

'Pooh, what a stink in here.'

It was a jar of decaying bluebells and their own seething bodies.

'Not much doubt about the source of infection in this village.'

Hands were tearing at the burnt-out furniture, feet shuffling through the rushes on the floor.

'She must live in the dark ages.'

'Burn her as a witch then. What's this then? Ouch! Stinging nettles in the saucepan!'

Miss Jigger thudded against the door.

'Somebody's upstairs.'

They looked towards the dark stairs.

'Smoke them out like rats like Mrs Slim said.'

'Oh, I didn't mean ...'

'Wet newspaper. Who's got some wet newspaper?'

Nobody.

'Light the bulrushes. Stand back everybody.'

She struck a match. Flame ran at the side of the green reed and died.

'Try the brown ones.'

They crowded behind her, straining floral hocks, as match after match flickered from her fingers.

'It's caught. Get back.'

She lumbered backwards from the heap of smoking rushes, pushing the others through the door and closing it.

'They'll shoot down those stairs in a minute.'

Mrs Slim knelt to raise Miss Jigger and as she leant her against the wall the beige jacket fell open, and she felt the soft flop of her body in its nylon harnesses and drew back.

'Shouldn't something be done about her head? And that poor cyclist?'

The cyclists hung about the garden unable to believe that this crowd of women was not going to nurse their injured leader.

'What's keeping those kids?'

'They'll be down in a minute. It's smoking nicely.'

'Won't somebody help this poor woman?' pleaded Mrs Slim. 'She's barely conscious.'

'Nobody's stopping you,' several people pointed out and she was forced to kneel again and dab the vast forehead and clogged eyebrows with her own handkerchief. She went into the kitchen, holding her hand over her mouth against the smoke, took a cup and turned on the tap: a rusty shriek and a flake of rust fell into the cup. A floorboard was smouldering. She went out.

'Any sign of those kids?'

'No, and I think you ought to put that fire out, it's taking hold.'

'Hark at her.'

She removed her handkerchief from Miss Jigger's fist and turned to the cyclist's extended leg.

Paula, Ralph and Stephen came up the lane to find their garden blocked with bicycles and youths in shorts, crawling children and prams and waiting women and Mrs Slim ministering to a great knee, and all were watching grey smoke from the empty kitchen window-frame, except Miss Jigger who lay with closed eyes. They ran round the house and into the field behind it. Ralph and Paula climbed a low hawthorn to watch. Stephen, abandoned at the foot of the trunk, saw a dark wavering in the water at his feet and alarmed eyes watching fishes flicking through the feathery grass.

'Sssh.'

A shout came from the blossom and Ralph and Paula splashed down beside them.

'They're going.'

Dennis stood up and saw the bicycles disappearing with rigid flags in the evening and the prams toil back up the lane. A figure darted back, the smoke bulged out of the window, dispersed and faded and the figure came out and ran down the lane in a hysterical knock-kneed sprint in the opposite direction from the prams. Last of all two people, one with a hand clasped to her brow, the other hopping on one foot, came out leaning heavily on a bicycle and were carried down the slope towards the river.

'Where's your brother gone?'

'To see if our chicken's come back.'

'I've got the hen at home. I told your mother I'd take you back there to wait for her.'

He took a hand in each of his and they walked

towards the fence, Ralph backwards because he had taken the wrong hand. When they reached the garden Stephen insisted on waiting for his mother in the hen-house. After ten minutes pleading Dennis braced an angry shoulder to overturn the shed and stepped back.

'Oh leave him,' said Paula and Dennis punched the wire netting window and strode up the garden, water still spurting from his shoes. At the front gate Paula hung back and said she was staying with Stephen.

'You're coming with me.' Dennis dragged them both after him through the gate and their heads collided. A cheerful song came from the bottom of the garden, but the blow on the window had dislodged the latch and it had fallen.

Ralph started to cry.

'Oh you make me sick, the whole damn lot of you,' shouted Dennis, tearing his hands from theirs and stalking off the way he had seen Coral go.

He found her by the river staring into a hole in the opposite bank.

'Coral.'

He jumped down beside her and pulled her round to face him.

'The children?'

'They're all right.'

'I'll get back then.'

'No.'

'Let go.'

'What do you want of me then?'

'I've never wanted anything from you. I want to be sufficient unto myself, like a tree, quietly rotting away.'

'Coral, you're twenty-four years old.'

She stood and he saw tiny beads of blood sparkling up her leg. She turned and walked away across the field.

● ● ●

A car stopped outside the cottage and a lady got out and entered the kitchen.

'I'm Jane Condor,' she introduced herself to the two hostile faces barring the door. 'I'm from the children's department. You must look on me as a sort of proxy mummy for the moment, till we get things sorted out.'

Paula had dredged out her old glasses and put them on, squinting up through a smeared lens.

'Did your mother take your little brother with her?' Jane Condor asked kindly, removing the hand that was picking at the Elastoplast over the lens.

'Drop dead.' Miss Condor saw that she was a case for a special school.

In his cage at the bottom of the garden Stephen heard the back door close, saw a scarlet knee propel Paula and Ralph through the gate, heard a car start and drive away, and was left in the silence of feathers and lime while the disturbed air drifted back.

Dennis sat aching in his wet clothes, watching the brown water for ten minutes before he stood up stiffly and followed her across the field, running when he saw her poise for a second on a stile, then jump into nothingness.

A wood loomed in front of her, suffused with gloom from the sky.

'Coral,' he called, crashing into brambles, clinging to a dead tree as lumps of chalk slid under his feet. His bleating strayed among the trees. A bird fluttered in the dead leaves – he turned – no one. He chose himself a stout staff, which broke beneath his weight, and started home through the sparse wood, up the corrupt chalk cliff with hanging roots and cobwebs, where someone pulling a rock-rose might find himself hurtling with a boulder in his hand to a bed of tyres and rusty tins, and a car buried to its roof in leaves. 'It is anybody's guess,' he thought, 'how many missing persons rot in Kentish leaves.' He came out of the wood into a sloping field and saw Filston below him but no sign of Coral.

A cow lifted her head from the tank where she was drinking and stared at him, a silver stream of water was rolling down her chin and her tail swinging at a cloud of flies. More long-horned cows who lay in the grass and looked at each other rose to their feet. Dennis started walking confidently down the field, heard thudding behind him and broke into a run, tripped, rolled down the hill and collided with a pair of skidding hooves that churned buttercups into his face. He sat up with his chin bleeding again and saw a brown dewlap swinging across his eyes and crawled a few inches, dreading the clamp of those great soft lips. The cow stood against the gate. Dennis backed slowly along the fence but it was parallel to a deep ditch of nettles. He faced her inward curving horns, took a few steps back and galloped at her, waving his arms and shouting, 'Shooo!' Flies buzzed at the corners of her calm eyes, the other cows were closing in on him.

'Excuse me.' He ventured to touch the heaving side but the hooves were firmly planted. Dennis sank down in the field and took a mouthful of grass.

*　　*　　*

When Coral came out of the wood she had wandered homewards between resting cows' heads by a different path. Blundering feet crashed faintly in the wood behind her.

She came to the sunken garden of Henton House and, in crossing the rotting canal bed, she grasped a branch of guelder-rose to steady her feet on the slimy weir. It slipped through her fingers leaving her swaying on the stone with a snowball of petals in her hand. Fear of the stinking mud below drove her across with wildly waving arms, and when she landed in the grass fear for the children struck her like lightning and she tore burning through the rising white mist and birdsong until she flung herself against a fence of high stakes at the far end of the grounds. She placed one foot on the wire running along halfway and pulled herself up, placed a foot on the points of two stakes and jumped. Her hair swung across her face and lassoed a stake. She was jerked backwards choking, hair ripping, feet fighting for the wire. The fence creaked under her, the stake was uprooted and sagged back pulling her hair tighter. She pulled her head from side to side, tearing at her neck with one hand, holding on with the other. Her eyes strained at their sockets, her mouth hung open. Her bursting ears heard Elf trumpeting like a lost bull through the stinking gardens of Henton House.

As she hung there, her legs dangling from the flapping black dress, she was very little different from the old crow her father had nailed to the post so many years ago.

Other Titles by Shena Mackay
Available from Virago

MUSIC UPSTAIRS

'In *Music Upstairs* she tells the breathless tale of Sidonie
... It is scruffy, sweaty, shapeless, desultory, vivid, and
heavy with inchoate poetry of adolescence: a right rave
along the Earl's Court Road and boozers adjacent'
– *Daily Telegraph*

When Sidonie O'Neill and her friend Joyce move into a room in
Earl's Court, the neighbourliness of Pam and Lenny Beacon
seems too good to be true: the offer of an open larder and a flat
warm with drying washing promises a haven from shoe-string
meals and disorderly single life. Things take a different turn,
however, when both Pam and Lenny begin to court Sidonie's
affection. With the fecklessness of youth she becomes the lover of
each of them, unwilling to commit herself to either or to
withdraw. Her response to Pam is instant and assured, her
liaison with Lenny is an ambivalent one, an arrangement in
which afternoons of sex stave off the monotony of jobless days.
Caught in a state of limbo, Sidonie veers between the two,
heedless of the chaos around her and of Lenny's increasingly
obsessive behaviour . . .

DUST FALLS ON EUGENE SCHLUMBURGER/TODDLER ON THE RUN

'Both are macabre, zany, scoffingly dross, sadly beautiful, wildly funny, glitteringly stylish – and quite brilliant . . . She stands on her own – an original and a very hot property' – *Daily Mail*

These punchy, vivid novellas show Shena Mackay's inimitable skill in recording the lives of the urban dispossessed – the young women and men who kick against an authority that besieges them. Abigail pines for her lover during school assemblies where nuns preach sacrifice, but romance is snatched from them when he crashes the car stolen for their joy ride. With Eugene sent down for two years, she has ample opportunity to pursue adolescent angst and to contemplate his escape . . . Morris, twenty-three years old and only three feet nine inches tall, is often mistaken for a child, though the events that entangle him are far from childish. On the run from the law, he takes refuge in a beach hut with Leda. Camouflaged by donkey rides and festive holidaymakers, they scramble through the days, fortified by salty tea, beset with fear and desperation.

NOT THE END OF THE WORLD
Rebecca Stowe

'A distinctive and remarkable new voice' – *Shena Mackay*

Twelve-year-old Maggie Pittsfield must be the luckiest girl in
the world. She lives in a house with its own beach and her father
owns the local candy factory. But are the Pittsfields really the
perfect American family? What lies behind the mysterious and
traumatic incident involving Maggie and her teacher Mr
Howard? And what is Maggie evading when she escapes to the
woods where the prospect of an encounter with the elusive
Pervert seems much less frightening than the revelation that
waits for her at home?

THE LAST ROOM
Elean Thomas

'Memorable . . . Thomas' Jamaican speech both sings and stings' – *Observer*

What happens when Valerie 'Putus' Barton is solemnly charged by her mother, Miss Belle, with the task of being the Barton who must take the family forward from the 'last room' of slavery into the 'mansions of the world'? Born into the third generation of African-Jamaicans after the abolition of European slavery, Putus is thus entrusted with a life mission. And so she begins a series of migrations, from the parish of St Catherine in Jamaica to a decrepit rooming-house in Birmingham; from her family, her country and ultimately from herself.

WINNER OF THE 1991 RUTH HADDEN MEMORIAL PRIZE